THE
HUNGER GAMES

THE OFFICIAL ILLUSTRATED MOVIE COMPANION

by Kate Egan

Scholastic Press • New York

Published by Scholastic Press, an imprint of Scholastic Inc., *Publishers since 1920*. SCHOLASTIC, SCHOLASTIC PRESS, and associated logos are trademarks and/or registered trademarks of Scholastic Inc.

Library of Congress Cataloging-in-Publication Data available
ISBN 978-0-545-42290-1

10 9 8 7 6 5 4 3 2   12 13 14 15 16 17/0
Printed in the U.S.A.   08
First edition, March 2012

This book was designed by Rick DeMonico and Heather Barber

CONTENTS

PART 1

THE HISTORY OF *THE HUNGER GAMES*

"THE RULES OF THE HUNGER GAMES ARE SIMPLE. IN PUNISHMENT FOR THE UPRISING, EACH OF THE TWELVE DISTRICTS MUST PROVIDE ONE GIRL AND ONE BOY, CALLED TRIBUTES, TO PARTICIPATE. THE TWENTY-FOUR TRIBUTES WILL BE IMPRISONED IN A VAST OUTDOOR ARENA THAT COULD HOLD ANYTHING FROM A BURNING DESERT TO A FROZEN WASTELAND. OVER A PERIOD OF SEVERAL WEEKS, THE COMPETITORS MUST FIGHT TO THE DEATH. THE LAST TRIBUTE STANDING WINS."
— FROM *THE HUNGER GAMES*

An extraordinary girl is trapped inside a game of life and death. With no special training, no magic powers, she finds a way to survive — just like she always has. But now the world is watching, and she's playing with forces bigger than she knows. Where some find inspiration, others see rebellion. And so the girl discovers: In these games, nobody really wins.

With its twisting plot and constant suspense, Suzanne Collins's novel *The Hunger Games* is impossible to put down. It keeps you reading, breathless, until the final page. You're not alone if you stayed up half the night to finish it, racing toward the end.

But it's not just the storytelling that hooks you. It's that the central character, sixteen-year-old Katniss Everdeen, is at once so brave and so real. What carries her through the grueling challenges of the arena? What's her one goal, in this perverse place where violence leads to victory and love leads to defeat? She's not after wealth or fame — she just wants to get back home.

Katniss has a focus, a raw power, that ordinary people can only dream of. And yet, like us, she's not entirely in control of her own destiny. In our difficult times, Katniss is a heroine we can understand.

The Hunger Games and its sequels, *Catching Fire* and *Mockingjay*, have been on the top of bestseller lists for the last three years and counting. In the United States alone, there are sixteen million copies of these books in print. They've lured in readers young and old, become the basis for countless articles and fan sites, and inspired other artists.

Now, for the first time, fans of the series will see *The Hunger Games* brought to life on film.

It's a major motion picture in every sense of the word: major talent, major effort, major interest. This book will take you behind the scenes, from script to screen, casting to costumes, training to trees. Lots and lots of trees.

First, though, to the book's beginnings, the soul of the film . . .

I t all started when author Suzanne Collins was up way too late one night, sitting on her couch and watching TV. She was flipping channels, switching between a reality show and news coverage of the Iraq war, when suddenly the images began to blur in her mind.

On one channel, young people were testing their limits and going to extremes to entertain an audience. On another channel, young people were fighting for their country and risking their lives.

An idea began to form.

What if a group of kids was required to fight — and risk their lives — as entertainment? Who would be watching? What would this show look like? Could anybody win these games? And what would happen if they did? Suzanne Collins was in the middle of writing a different book, but these questions lingered in her imagination.

It had been five years since Collins had followed a friend's advice and tried her hand at writing a children's book. Her first novel, *Gregor the Overlander*, was about an eleven-year-old boy who

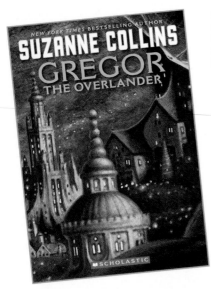

LEFT: SUZANNE'S FIRST NOVEL, *GREGOR THE OVERLANDER.* BELOW: AUTHOR SUZANNE COLLINS.

falls through a grate in the laundry room of his apartment building. Suddenly he finds himself in a strange world populated by giant cockroaches, spiders, bats, and rats — all the creatures you might expect to find beneath New York City. These species have coexisted uneasily for years, but their world is on the brink of war. Gregor can't wait to get out, until he discovers that his presence in this world, the Underland, has been foretold in a prophecy, and sticking around might just help him find his missing father. He embarks on a quest that will change both him and this strange land forever.

In 2003, *Gregor the Overlander* was published to wide acclaim, making Suzanne Collins an author to watch. Soon her publisher, Scholastic, signed up the next books in what she had always envisioned as a five-part series. By the time the third, *Gregor and the Curse of the Warmbloods*, was published, the series had found a loyal following of readers. The series finale, *Gregor and the Code of Claw*, was a *New York Times* bestseller. With a hungry audience and a growing reputation for fast-paced, thought-provoking stories, Collins was poised to take her next step as a writer.

Most of her career had been spent in children's television, writing shows for Nickelodeon and PBS, like *Clarissa Explains It All*, *Oswald*, *Little Bear*, and *Clifford's Puppy Days*. Collins loved writing for young children, and several of her shows had been nominated for Emmy Awards, but she'd long been fascinated by subjects more suitable for older kids.

In *The Underland Chronicles* (as the *Gregor* books came to be known), Collins had created a complex society that exploded into war. Her readers were mostly in middle school, but she had written genocide and biological weapons into these books. She had killed off beloved characters to explore the cost and the emotional fallout of war. Still, she had more to say about when and how — or whether — war could be justified. In a young adult novel, she might delve more deeply into the subject. While waiting for editorial comments on her final *Gregor* book, Collins wrote a short proposal for a young adult trilogy called *The Hunger Games*.

Collins found inspiration in several places beyond her TV set. First, in her childhood love of Greek mythology, particularly the story of Theseus and the Minotaur. As part of the surrender terms of a war, King Minos of Crete required that the city of Athens send tribute to him in the form of seven youths and seven maidens. These tributes went into a labyrinth to face the Minotaur — half man and half monster — who would then destroy them all. This savagery continued until the Athenian prince, Theseus, went as tribute to Crete, and killed the Minotaur instead.

OTHER PARENTS TRIED TO SHELTER THEIR KIDS FROM THE IDEA OF WAR, BUT COLLINS'S FATHER CHALLENGED HIS KIDS TO ASK QUESTIONS. WHAT, IF ANYTHING, MADE THESE BLOODY BATTLES WORTH THEIR COST?

As a child, Suzanne Collins was struck by the cruelty of the Cretan king, and it stayed in the back of her mind as she began to construct the country of Panem, the setting for *The Hunger Games*. Like King Minos, Panem's cold and calculating President Snow sends a clear message to his people. As Collins puts it: "Mess with us and we'll do something worse than kill you. We'll kill your children."

One of Collins's favorite movies is the classic *Spartacus*, based on the true story of a Roman slave. While being trained in a gladiator school, Spartacus

and his mates overthrew their guards and escaped to freedom. Led by Spartacus, they were joined by other slaves, and the rebellion built to the Third Servile War with the Roman Empire. Like Katniss, Spartacus followed a path from slave to gladiator, from gladiator to rebel, and from rebel to the face of a war.

Most important, all of Collins's ideas for the trilogy were steeped in the war stories she heard as a child. Her father had spent his entire career in the Air Force, as a military specialist as well as a historian and a doctor of political science. He served in Vietnam when Collins was six, and moved the family between the US and Europe for his work after he returned. War was never far from his mind, and he had a unique gift for making the subject come alive for his four children.

The Collins family visited many battlefields, and Collins's father never shied away from telling his kids what had happened there. He told them what led to the battle, what happened in the battle, and what its consequences were for the real people who fought in it and the citizens whose futures depended on its outcome. Other parents tried to shelter their kids from the idea of war, but Collins's father challenged his kids to ask questions. What, if anything, made these bloody battles worth their cost? Collins knew only too well what it meant to wait and worry for a parent who might never come home.

All of these pieces went into the proposal, which she sent out in the summer of 2006. The three-and-a-half-page write-up included an overview of the Games and brief descriptions of each book. "Although set in the future," Collins wrote, "*The Hunger Games* explores disturbing issues of modern warfare such as who fights our wars, how they are orchestrated, and the ever-increasing opportunities to observe them being played out." She also noted that Katniss, though "distrustful," has "a deep capacity to love and sacrifice for those few people

THE TRIBUTES PAY CLOSE ATTENTION TO ATALA (KARAN KENDRICK) DURING THEIR FIRST DAY IN THE TRAINING CENTER.

she cares for." The final books have hewn closely to the original outlines — except for the titles. The original working title for the first book in the trilogy was *The Tribute of District Twelve.*

On the strength of those few pages, Scholastic snapped up the right to publish the *Hunger Games* trilogy.

"When I sat down to write this series, I assumed it would be like *The Underland Chronicles*," Collins told the *New York Times* later. "Written in the third person and the past tense. I began writing, and the words came out not only in the first person, in the present tense, in Katniss's voice. It was almost as if the character was insisting on telling the story herself. So I never really make a concentrated effort to get inside her head; she was already very much alive in mine."

The publisher knew it had something special on its hands as soon as Collins turned in her first draft. Editorial director David Levithan says, "I remember that the manuscript came in on a Friday, and I read it over the weekend. Two other people read it — Kate Egan, Suzanne's longtime editor, and Jennifer Rees, an editor who was also working on the books. On Monday morning, we were dying to talk to each other — it was simply one of the most astonishing things we'd ever read. Our editorial conversation pretty much consisted of one word: *Wow.*"

Everyone involved knew the best way to sell the book was to get people to read it. First up were the people in Scholastic's sales, marketing, and publicity departments, who were blown away and started off the buzzstorm. Advance reader's copies went out and were devoured in one sitting by booksellers and librarians. Scholastic announced a first printing of 50,000 copies . . . and then doubled it . . . and then doubled it again, as the buzz got louder and louder. Suzanne's literary agent, Rosemary Stimola, began selling foreign rights to publishers across the world. To date, it has sold in 45 territories. When *The Hunger Games* was published in October 2008, it met with resounding praise.

The first reviews came from book-industry magazines like *Publishers Weekly* and *Booklist*, and every one of them was a rave. *Horn Book* said, "Collins has written a compulsively readable blend of science fiction, survival story, unlikely romance, and social commentary."

School Library Journal agreed, writing, "Collins's characters are completely realistic and sympathetic as they form alliances and friendships in the face of overwhelming odds; the plot is tense, dramatic, and engrossing. This book will definitely resonate with the generation raised on reality shows like *Survivor* and *American Gladiator*."

As *The Hunger Games* began to climb to the top of bestseller lists, other bestselling authors began to weigh in.

In *Entertainment Weekly*, Stephen King reviewed *The Hunger Games*, calling it, "A violent, jarring, speed-rap of a novel that generates nearly constant suspense. . . . I couldn't stop reading. . . . Collins is an efficient no-nonsense prose stylist with a pleasantly

> "OUR EDITORIAL CONVERSATION PRETTY MUCH CONSISTED OF ONE WORD: *WOW*."

dry sense of humor. Reading *The Hunger Games* is as addictive (and as violently simple) as playing one of those shoot-it-if-it-moves videogames in the lobby of the local eightplex; you know it's not real, but you

PRODUCER NINA JACOBSON ON SET IN NORTH CAROLINA.

keep plugging in quarters anyway . . ."

Stephenie Meyer loved it, too, and as the author of the *Twilight* series, she knew what it was like to be a sensation. She wrote, "I was so obsessed with this book I had to take it with me out to dinner and hide it under the edge of the table so I wouldn't have to stop reading. The story kept me up for several nights in a row, because even after I was finished, I just lay in bed wide awake thinking about it. . . . *The Hunger Games* is amazing."

The response to the book was more than anyone involved had dared to hope for.

Two months after it was published, *The Hunger Games* was on several best-of-the-year book lists. It was catching on with teens and adults alike — it was even being taught in schools. Collins visited a middle school in Plainfield, Illinois, soon after *The Hunger Games* was published. Its students created a tribute parade in the gym, and Collins did her presentation in front of a large inflatable Cornucopia. Later, a silver parachute was lowered by pulley from the ceiling — containing the mockingjay necklace that Collins wears to this day. The enthusiasm at the school was as contagious as the enthusiasm in newspapers, magazines, and online.

Naturally, *The Hunger Games* had begun to capture the attention of Hollywood.

Film producer Nina Jacobson, of Color Force Productions, had overseen movies like *The Princess Diaries*, *The Chronicles of Narnia*, and the *Pirates of the Caribbean* series. She describes her first encounter with *The Hunger Games*: "A smart guy who works for me, named Bryan Unkeless, read the book and fell in love with it. Just the first book had been published — the sequels hadn't come out yet. He read it, and he gave it to me and said, 'It's a really great book. You should check it out.' I just picked it up, couldn't put it down, and spent a lot of the time that I was reading it thinking, *How can you make a movie that has violence between young people?* And yet, as I saw the way that Suzanne had walked that line, by staying inside Katniss's character and managing to comment on the violence without ever exploiting it, I became more convinced there was a way that a movie could do the same."

Many production companies were vying for a chance to make the movie version of her story. Collins put off making any decision until she had finished promoting *The Hunger Games* and writing its sequel, *Catching Fire*, but eventually she had a series of phone meetings with interested producers. "It's the major choice you make as an author,"

Collins says. "I was looking to get a feel for who they were, how they operated, what their priorities and game plan might be for a movie."

Jacobson knew that other producers were approaching Collins, which made her even more determined to make the movie herself. "I became pretty much obsessed with the book and then couldn't bear the thought that anybody else would produce the film."

Her pitch to Collins hit a nerve. "I made a very passionate case to Suzanne that there were versions of her book, as a movie, that she could really hate and that would end up being sort of guilty of the crimes of the Capitol. There could be a version of the movie which stylized and glamorized the violence, where the movie became, say, the Hunger Games. I felt that an ethical version of the movie needed to be made and needed to be safeguarded. And I felt very passionately about doing that and felt very confident that I could do that. And so I was able to win her over."

Collins says, "There were so many great choices, but ultimately I felt that Nina had the

"IT WASN'T ANYTHING CONTROVERSIAL THAT DREW US TO *THE HUNGER GAMES* — IT WAS THE IRRESISTIBLE CHARACTER OF KATNISS. EARLY ON, WE HAD A CLEAR SENSE OF WHAT OUR PRIORITIES WOULD BE . . . IT WAS ABOUT HER CHARACTER AND OUR CONNECTION TO HER STORY."

greatest connection to the work. I believed her when she said she would do everything she could to protect its integrity. And the fact that we had a mutual friend [novelist and screenwriter Peter Hedges] — who spoke so highly of her — tipped the scales in her favor."

The next step was to find a movie studio, and again there were many competing for the option.

Alli Shearmur, president of production at Lionsgate, recalls, "When Nina Jacobson got the opportunity to produce *The Hunger Games*, she called me and I read the book right away. I knew it would be worthwhile because it was from Nina — I have known her for a long time and always admired her. I read the book soon after it was published, before it was so well-known, so I was responding to the central story of Katniss, not to the cultural phenomenon that it has become. Of course I loved it, from beginning to end."

She shared the book with Joe Drake, president of Lionsgate's motion picture group, and Tim Palen, the company's president of marketing. They had questions about how the book would translate into film, but by the time they spoke to Suzanne Collins, they shared a clear vision.

Drake, who runs the motion picture group at the studio, explains that "Lionsgate is known for fearlessness — we have never shied away from bold projects that stir up conversation. But we don't make projects simply because they're edgy — whatever the genre, first and foremost we are always looking for quality stories that are character driven. So it wasn't anything controversial that drew us to *The Hunger Games* — it was the irresistible character of Katniss. Early on, we had a clear sense of what our priorities would be when telling the story . . . it was about her character and our connection to her story."

While Collins was finishing her first draft of *Mockingjay*, Jacobson met with many studios — including Lionsgate — and eventually came to feel that Lionsgate was the best choice for *The Hunger Games*.

Jacobson says, "I felt that Lionsgate really understood the material and that they would let us make a faithful adaptation; that they wouldn't soften it, they wouldn't age up the characters, to make them older so that it would be more palatable. I felt that the power of the book was in the youth of these protagonists and that you couldn't cheat on that in terms of their age in the story. Lionsgate was on board for, of course, the PG-13 version of the movie, not something full of blood and guts, but something more thematically driven."

The intense interest in her book still felt slightly unreal to Collins, and she had some practical reasons for feeling comfortable with Lionsgate. "Everyone we needed to get the movie going was right there on the phone," she remembers. "The studio was small enough for that to be possible. I agreed with Nina that this was probably the best home for the story, our best chance of seeing it made into a film."

At that point — with *Mockingjay* finished but not yet published — Collins began to develop the first draft of a script. She'd been writing scripts since she was twenty years old, and making a living as a writer since she was twenty-eight, so in some respects adapting her own work brought her back into familar territory. It also meant making some difficult choices.

Collins says, "There were several significant differences from writing the book. Time, for starters. When you're adapting a novel into a two-hour movie you can't bring everything with you. So a lot of compression is needed. Not all the characters are

don't think that the choices damaged the emotional arc of the story.

"Then there's the question of how best to take a book told in the first person and transform it into a satisfying dramatic experience. In the novel, you never leave Katniss for a second and are privy to all of her thoughts. We needed to find ways to dramatize her inner world and to make it possible for other characters to exist outside of her company without letting the audience get ahead of her.

"Finally, there's the challenge of how to present the violence while still maintaining a PG-13 rating so that your core audience can view it. A lot of things that are acceptable on a page have to be handled very carefully on a screen. But that's ultimately the director's job."

Soon veteran screenwriter Billy Ray, director and writer of acclaimed films like *Breach* and *Shattered Glass*, came on board to further develop the script. Lionsgate's Alli Shearmur says, "We thought that the bridge to the movie could be explored even further by someone who'd done this many times," and Collins adds, "He was a complete pleasure to work with. Amazingly talented, collaborative, and always respectful of the book." Then, off the strength of this revised script, Lionsgate went to directors.

There was no shortage of interested directors reading the script, people with great talent and experience. Once a director was chosen, Collins

"MANY DIRECTORS WERE INTERESTED, BUT [GARY ROSS] BLEW US AWAY WITH HIS PRESENTATION. HE'D MADE A DOCUMENTARY TO SHOW US — INTERVIEWS WITH FRIENDS OF HIS TEENAGE CHILDREN, TALKING ABOUT WHAT *THE HUNGER GAMES* MEANT TO THEM."

going to make it to the screen. For example, we gave up Madge, cut the Avox girl's backstory, and reduced the Career pack. It was hard to let them go but I

knew that person's vision would be the guiding force behind the project. Color Force and Lionsgate interviewed potential directors, hoping to find one with

a vision that would complement Collins's. Before long, the team found that person in Gary Ross, the Oscar®-nominated writer and director known for movies like *Big*, *Dave*, *Pleasantville*, and *Seabiscuit*.

Ross's teenage twins had read the book first, and they raved about it. "I mentioned *The Hunger Games* to my kids, and they exploded, went on and on, and I had to actually stop them from telling me the entire story," Ross says. "So I went upstairs, started reading around ten o'clock at night, and finished around one-thirty in the morning. I literally put the book down and said, 'I have to make this movie. I just have to.' I got on a plane Monday morning and flew to England to see Nina Jacobson."

Jacobson was in London, making another movie, when Ross arrived in town and made reservations for dinner. "We sat down and we had a two-hour meal in which his understanding of the themes and the characters — the way that Katniss's point of view is the heart and soul of the story — was so spot-on," she says. "He just felt it so deeply. He understood the epic nature of the story and the intimate nature of the story. He was clear that he didn't want to make a sentimental movie, but it was important to him that the action comes from the characters, it doesn't just happen to the characters. Gary had great ideas for the movie visually, but we always knew he would come from a character place."

"Katniss understands the truth so clearly," Ross says. "That's why she can't tolerate tyrants, and that's what ultimately gives her the ability to rebel. She lives her own truth and she's very clear about who she is, about what is right and what is wrong. Kids hook into this character not just because she's kick-ass — though she is. They hook into this character because she's complicated, too. She's wrestling with a lot of things that a girl her age would wrestle with, just under incredibly urgent circumstances."

Alli Shearmur will never forget her first meeting with Gary Ross about *The Hunger Games*. "After Gary met with Nina in London, he came to Lionsgate to convince us he was the right director for the film. Many directors were interested, but he blew us away with his presentation. He'd made a documentary to show us — interviews with friends of his teenage children, talking about what *The Hunger Games* meant to them. He showed examples of the filmmaking style he'd want to use to tell Katniss's story. He even brought artwork to show what he imagined the film could look like. It was an electric presentation."

Suzanne Collins tells what happened next. "As part of Gary's creative process, he wrote a subsequent draft which incorporated his incredible directorial vision of the film. And then he very generously invited me in to work with him on it. We had an immediate and exhilarating creative connection that brought the script to the first day of shooting."

"I've had great relationships with all the authors I've adapted," Ross says. "But with Suzanne it was very special because we ended up actual collaborators. It wasn't just that she was involved — it's that we became a writing team. We were always talking, we had a good relationship, but then she came to LA in person. I got her thoughts on the script, and her thoughts were so good that we began writing together before we even realized it. It was important to me that she be involved, and it felt so natural and spontaneous that it was a wonderful thing."

Meanwhile, the cast of the movie was beginning to come together.

Nina Jacobson recalls her first thoughts about casting the movie. "Once people knew a movie was going to come out, then people got very opinionated about who should play the roles and obviously that's a lot of pressure. But I think a book adaptation doesn't have to be just like the book, it has to feel like the book. That's what you want. You want to get the feeling from the movie that you got from the book, and you want the characters to evoke the characters that you fell in love with. And so it was really a matter of looking for the essence of each character in each actor, knowing we can manipulate hair color, we can manipulate a lot of things, but we can't really change somebody's essence."

"It was definitely a different casting process than I'd ever been through before," Gary Ross comments. "The fan base feels incredibly connected to the story and everybody had a visceral sense of who should play these characters. People are connected to the material — for them it's personal."

Veteran casting director Debra Zane cast a wide net for actors to play the main parts, but the production team also had some intriguing ideas of their own. "The loudest, most influential voice in the casting was Gary's," says Alli Shearmur of Lionsgate.

Producer Jon Kilik was working with Nina Jacobson and Gary Ross, and he was a part of many early conversations about casting. "I had seen *Winter's Bone* and I didn't want to influence Gary," he says. "But when Gary mentioned Jennifer Lawrence, it literally sent shivers up my spine because I thought she was so perfect."

"We all knew it was about Katniss first and once you found her, then you could find everybody else," executive producer Robin Bissell adds. "So

> "YOU WANT TO GET THE FEELING FROM THE MOVIE THAT YOU GOT FROM THE BOOK, AND YOU WANT THE CHARACTERS TO EVOKE THE CHARACTERS THAT YOU FELL IN LOVE WITH."

Katniss was our focus. From the start we talked about Jennifer Lawrence, but we couldn't just say we're only going to see one person. So we had a lot of people come in and read, but we were still thinking about Jennifer on some level."

Twenty-year-old actress Jennifer Lawrence had only one starring role to her credit, but it had earned

her an Academy Award® nomination for best actress. Her performance as Ree in *Winter's Bone* had catapulted her out of obscurity, startling audiences with its raw intensity. Lawrence was blonde and beautiful, a few years older than Katniss Everdeen — she wasn't an obvious match for the role. And yet she'd been completely believable as a destitute teenager living in the Ozarks. Ross, Jacobson, Lionsgate, and Collins were eager to give her a chance.

Lawrence remembers reading *The Hunger Games* for the first time. "I read the books around Christmas [2010], and I went through them all in a matter of days. I just thought they were amazing. I loved the futuristic Joan of Arc character of Katniss. And it's hard to say that something in the future is 'true,' but the book speaks truly about our time — it's incredibly relevant."

At first she wasn't sure how she felt about seeing the books in movie form. "I was skeptical because I loved the books so much, but when I met with Gary Ross I realized within about thirty seconds that he was the only one who could make the movie and make it in the right way."

With great confidence in Ross's team, Lawrence read for the highly coveted lead role of Katniss. From the moment she walked into the room, her presence was magnetic. Nina Jacobson remembers, "There was instant power and intensity and certainty in Jen's performance. She came in with this great understanding of this character. This is actually a girl whose fierceness comes from a nurturing place, not a conquering place. In her audition we used the scene in which she's saying good-bye to her mother and her sister and Gale. There's a line in the scene in which she tells her mother, 'Don't cry.' And just in the way she tells her mom 'Don't cry,' it's kind of like 'Don't you dare cry. Don't you dare fall apart in this situation.' In that one little moment, she spoke volumes

about this character and her past and her present and her future."

Gary Ross adds, "I've worked with amazing actors. Someone like Jen comes by once in a generation. I mean, this is an unbelievably rare thing. This is Michael Jordan, this is Baryshnikov, this talent is almost stunning to witness. There's nothing you can ask her to do that she can't do."

Lionsgate's Joe Drake reminisces about the audition tape that landed Lawrence the unanimous support of the studio, and ultimately the role: "We always factor in a certain degree of research and analysis when we make these major casting decisions. But what ultimately led us to cast Jennifer in the role of Katniss wasn't anything that could be calculated — it was the visceral reaction of myself and the other decision makers at Lionsgate to her audition. Jennifer's read gave me chills, and it made me cry. At the end of the day, all of the best casting decisions are made based on raw talent and gut reactions, and we are particularly proud of this one."

Jennifer Lawrence was in London when she heard she'd landed the part and was overjoyed and overwhelmed: "I was convinced I didn't have it. And then I got the phone call while I was in London.

JENNIFER LAWRENCE LOSES HERSELF IN A BOOK WHILE TAKING A BREAK FROM SHOOTING A SCENE IN THE TRAINING CENTER.

I was then terrified. I knew this was going to be huge, and that was scary. I called my mom. She said, 'This is a script that you love, and you're thinking about not doing it because of the size of it?' And I don't want to not do something because I'm scared, so I said yes to the part, and I'm so happy I did."

Suzanne Collins had been in on the audition, and she was one of the first people to set Lawrence's mind at ease about the role. She drove it home to Lawrence that it didn't matter if people said she was too old or too blonde to play Katniss. "I talked to Suzanne after I got the part, when I was still in England, and it was incredible — I mean, I'm her biggest fan. She said, 'I know you can do it,' and all of these other nice things that just gave me the boost that I needed. Hearing them from the woman who created Katniss — I felt like a huge weight had been lifted off my shoulders," Lawrence recalls.

"And then we moved on to Peeta and Gale," says Robin Bissell, "and it was almost exactly the same thing. Josh came in and he sat down and read the cave scene, where he's hurt and Katniss is nursing him back to life, and immediately he was Peeta. I mean, it was that clear."

Jacobson says, "When Josh Hutcherson came in to audition, I had actually just met with him earlier

in the week, and he was so comfortable in his own skin, so charming and so at ease and so likeable. I felt that he really captured that 'Peeta-ocity' of somebody who seemed genuinely sweet, genuinely likeable, but also that he could be a little smooth when he needed to be. You could see how he could cover the politician side of the character that Katniss is both attracted to and suspicious of."

Suzanne Collins put it this way to *Entertainment Weekly*: "If Josh had been bright purple and had had six foot wings and gave that audition, I'd have been like, 'Cast him! We can work around the wings!' He was that good."

Josh Hutcherson had been working as an actor for almost a decade already. He had appeared in classic children's movies like *The Polar Express* and *Bridge to Terabithia*; as he grew, so did the depth of his roles. When Gary Ross and the producers were

> "IF JOSH HAD BEEN BRIGHT PURPLE AND HAD HAD SIX FOOT WINGS AND GAVE THAT AUDITION, I'D HAVE BEEN LIKE, 'CAST HIM! WE CAN WORK AROUND THE WINGS!' HE WAS THAT GOOD."

considering him, Hutcherson had recently played a key part in the acclaimed movie *The Kids Are All Right*, with Julianne Moore and Annette Bening. Starring in *The Hunger Games*, though, would change the course of his career.

Hutcherson says, "I fell in love with Peeta right away. His self-deprecating humor, his outlook on life, and how he doesn't want things to change him — those things are really a part of who I am as a person. I've been in this business since I was nine years old and that can change you. Staying true to who I am, and what my value system is, has been

JOSH HUTCHERSON AS LASER IN *THE KIDS ARE ALL RIGHT* (2010).

important to me since I was really young."

There was an immediate rapport between Lawrence and Hutcherson, according to many people involved in the casting. Jon Kilik says, "Jennifer and Josh have gotten along great from the beginning, right when they met in rehearsals and even in the casting process. There was a real connection there. They're both from Kentucky, very close to where District Twelve is supposed to be. So there was this common bond, and it just grew from there."

The final part of the pivotal trio was put in place with the casting of Australian actor Liam Hemsworth as Gale. Hemsworth had recently drawn attention as the love interest of Miley Cyrus in *The Last Song*. He wouldn't have a great deal of screen time in *The Hunger Games*, but Ross and the producers were already looking ahead to future movies, where Gale would step into the spotlight.

Jacobson puts it this way: "Liam is this big, hunky guy. He has a clear physical advantage over Peeta, which we found interesting — that they would be physically contrasting types. And when we put the actors together in the auditions, you could see how, when Katniss asks Gale to take care of her family, she would trust that he'd do it. Liam is able

GALE (LIAM HEMSWORTH)

GALE CARRIES A CRYING PRIM (WILLOW SHIELDS) AWAY FROM THE REAPING. HE PROMISES KATNISS THAT HE'LL LOOK OUT FOR HER FAMILY WHILE SHE'S GONE.

to communicate very effectively with his eyes and with the small gestures. But you also believe that he has that revolutionary spirit, that he has that fiery quality inside of him."

Like Jennifer Lawrence, Liam Hemsworth had a great relationship with Josh Hutcherson. The two would be rivals in the film, but not in real life. Hemsworth says, "I was friends with him before this, and he's a great actor. He's one of the smartest people I've ever met, too. Honestly, I'll listen to him talk sometimes and it's like I feel he could lead us into a battle, and I'd follow him. He's that persuasive."

Jacobson also noticed their chemistry. "We sent the two guys into training and they got really into it, really gonzo. They got to be very good friends during the training process."

With the three central characters cast, Ross moved toward casting the key adult supporting roles.

Elizabeth Banks, an actress known for her roles in the *Spider-Man* trilogy, *Seabiscuit*, and *30 Rock*, was immediately interested. She says, "I called everyone I knew the minute I heard they were making a movie of it. Gary and I worked together on *Seabiscuit*, so when he got the directing job I sent him a little e-mail like, 'Just so you know, I'll totally play Effie!' It was a dream of mine from the get-go."

Ross had a dual vision for the role of Effie Trinket, Katniss's escort to the Capitol, and not just anyone would be able to pull it off. "We wanted an actress who could have the comedic chops," explains Jacobson, "but also the dramatic undertones. Somebody who could do a lot with a little, because there's a version of Effie that could be very over-the-top, very distracting. The person needs to be ridiculous in some ways and yet have a reality to her. Elizabeth Banks, we felt, brought all of that to the table."

And Banks was not the only actor actively pursuing a part in the film. Film legend Donald Sutherland, a fixture in movies and on television

for the better part of six decades, wrote a letter to his agent and Lionsgate indicating that he'd like to play Panem's President Snow. "Though the part that I play is, in the first book, small, the film can be so significant in reaching young people and teaching them how to deal with the oligarchy of the privileged, the hegemony of capitalism, it is a revolutionary piece of work. I'm thrilled with it." Plus, "I wanted to work with Gary Ross," continues Sutherland. "He's a brilliant, brilliant writer and, working with him, you discover that he's a perfect director."

Executive producer Robin Bissell says, "Gary was like, 'Okay . . . you know it's just a couple of days. It's not that much — you do a speech and that's it.' But Donald said, 'No, I really want to do

it.' I think he knew that this character becomes the embodiment of the Capitol, and he saw what he could do with it. Donald came in toward the end of shooting and he wrote another letter to Gary

> "[EFFIE]'S THE COMIC RELIEF IN A LOT OF WAYS. SHE'S A VERY FLAMBOYANT PERSON. BUT SHE'S ALSO, I THINK, VERY SCARED."
> — ELIZABETH BANKS

afterward — he had some ideas and very eloquent thoughts on President Snow. Immediately after Gary read the letter, he said, 'I have ideas for two

more scenes'— scenes between Snow and Seneca Crane. Seneca isn't thinking about the ultimate reason for the Games. For him, it's about ratings, it's about showbiz. But Snow never loses sight of what the Games are about. So . . . Donald Sutherland brought a great deal to this part."

Gary Ross remembers it like this: "So, we're shooting in the woods by the edge of this lake, and I read this e-mail from Donald and I was just knocked out. I went down by the lake and there was one folding chair sitting in this little clearing, and I thought, *Well, okay — this is a sign. Clearly I'm going to sit in this chair.* So I went over, I sat down, and I came up with these two scenes for Snow, which I think are really pivotal in the movie, and define him in a great way."

Ross and the producers sought out actors they thought were right for other parts, particularly Haymitch Abernathy, the only living victor from District 12, and Cinna, Katniss's brilliant stylist.

Of Haymitch, Jacobson explains, "We wanted a character who felt like he'd seen it all and experienced it all and had that weariness, on the one hand, but also that subversive, fiery unpredictability. We wanted somebody who could play the drunk without being really obvious about it, who could play that sort of broken clown, but really had the intelligence and the foresight and the strategy to get these two characters through these Games alive."

"We approached Woody Harrelson," continues Bissell. Harrelson's breakthrough role had been in the television series *Cheers*, and he'd gone on to earn two Oscar® nominations for his work in the films *The Messenger* and *The People vs. Larry Flynt*. "Woody loves Gary, really wanted to work with Gary. So he read the books, he read the script, and then he said, 'I get it. I have to do this movie.'"

When it came time to cast Cinna, the producers approached the gifted musician and singer-song-writer Lenny Kravitz. "Lenny as Cinna was an idea that Gary had very early on," says producer Jon Kilik. "He wanted Cinna to be not only a stylist but somebody who has a lot of style. And nobody in this world has more style, more charm, more charisma than Lenny Kravitz."

Kravitz, who had just appeared in the Oscar®-nominated film *Precious*, was delighted to join the team. "Gary Ross called me while I was in the studio recording my album, and said, 'I'm doing this

HAYMITCH (WOODY HARRELSON) RAISES A GLASS WHILE ON BOARD THE TRAIN TO THE CAPITOL.

movie, *The Hunger Games.* I'd like you to play the part of Cinna. And if you want the part, you've got it. You don't have to audition.' That was quite an amazing phone call, because I've only made a couple of films — it was just beautiful to get a role like that," Kravitz says.

The young actors playing the tributes came from many places and many backgrounds. Some were seasoned actors, with experience in television or commercials or smaller films, while others were complete unknowns. What they had in common was an enthusiasm for the film as well as a sense that this was a once-in-a-lifetime opportunity.

Alexander Ludwig was excited to get the role of Cato, a Career Tribute from District 2. He remembers really connecting with the role. "When I finally met Gary and he offered me the role of Cato, it was a no-brainer, because I was just such a big fan."

Isabelle Fuhrman, the actress who plays Clove, was passionate about the books long before getting cast in the movie. "*The Hunger Games* is my all-time

"GARY HAD A VISION OF CINNA AS BEING A GREAT ARTIST. AND IF YOU'RE A GREAT ARTIST IN AN OPPRESSIVE SOCIETY, WHAT CAN YOU DO? WHO ARE YOU? CAN YOU EXPRESS YOURSELF IN THE CAPITOL? PROBABLY NOT. AND SO YOU'RE THIS GUY WHO COMES AND PREPS TRIBUTES FOR THESE HORRIBLE GAMES." — ROBIN BISSELL

favorite book series, and I was the biggest book buff that you would ever possibly meet. I turned all my friends on to reading it. When I heard it was being made into a movie, I freaked out. I thought, *I have got to be in this movie.*"

Fuhrman originally auditioned for Katniss, but was told she was too young for the role. "I got a call a week later. They wanted me to audition for Clove. I read with Debra Zane, who's the sweetest person I've ever met." Fuhrman didn't have to wait long to find out if she got cast. She was at lunch with her mother when her agent called with the good news. She was so happy that she burst into tears. "People are staring, and I'm trying to make it seem like it's not a big deal, and I'm crying my eyes out, I'm so excited. Everyone was like, 'Who's this crazy little fourteen-year-old girl crying her eyes out at a vegan restaurant?'"

Jack Quaid, who plays Marvel, recalls, "The audition was kind of weird because it was the first audition I'd ever walked into where the first thing they said to me was 'Choose your weapon.' They had a box — there was a crossbow-y type thing, a big knife, and a gun. So I just picked up the big knife and I did the audition and, right about then, I knew this was going to be something cool. I go to NYU and I was in this class a few weeks later when I got the call that I got the part and I was flabbergasted. So . . . I'll have a unique story to tell about what I did with my summer vacation."

Twelve-year-old Amandla Stenberg's audition was a little different. "I went to Gary's house, and for the audition I'd actually dressed up and I'd been rolled around in dirt, like Rue in the Games. So I was all dressed with all my dirt and my leaves in my hair and everything, and when I got to Gary's house — well, he has a really nice house. I didn't want to sit on anything, because I didn't want to get anything dirty! I went in and I felt really good about

From right to left: Rue (Amandla Stenberg), District 4 Tribute Boy (Ethan Jamieson), Glimmer (Leven Rambin), District 3 Tribute Boy (Ian Nelson), Marvel (Jack Quaid), District 7 Tribute Girl (Leigha Hancock), Katniss (Jennifer Lawrence), District 8 Tribute Boy (Samuel Tan), Peeta (Josh Hutcherson), Foxface (Jacqueline Emerson), Clove (Isabelle Fuhrman), Thresh (Dayo Okeniyi), District 10 Tribute Boy (Jeremy Marinas), District 4 Tribute Girl (Tara Macken), District 5 Tribute Boy (Chris Mark), and Cato (Alexander Ludwig)

it, and then I got a call from my agent saying, 'What are you doing this summer?' and I was like, 'Not much. Why?' and she said, 'Because you booked *The Hunger Games*,' and I was screaming and squealing, 'I'm Rue!' and it was so exciting."

Jacqueline Emerson, who plays Foxface, re-members, "*The Hunger Games* was my all-school read at school, and I read the first book, and I just fell in love with the whole series. Then I found out there was gonna be a movie made of it, and I actu-

ally spent a whole day with my friends looking up those possible casts on YouTube. I was looking at people, being like, 'Oh, Emma Stone would make a great Foxface' — and now it's me!"

She continues, "I came in and I did an interview for Gary, because he was interviewing kids that had read the books. And I did that probably in the fall, and that was taped. And then, a couple of weeks later, he asked me if I wanted to come in and read for the role. I just completely freaked out!"

While the cast was still coming together, the central actors had already begun training — and training hard.

Nina Jacobson gives an overview of what Lawrence needed to do: "Obviously Katniss is a hunter. She's an archer, she has to be agile. You have to believe that this person could win the Hunger Games, and so we wanted her to have the skills, we wanted her to feel at home doing all of the things that Katniss does."

KATNISS RUNS THROUGH THE WOODS OUTSIDE DISTRICT 12.

PEETA MELLARK
OUTSIDE HIS
FAMILY'S BAKERY
IN DISTRICT 12.

FILMING IN THE ARENA. LEFT TO RIGHT: CLOVE (ISABELLE FUHRMAN), PEETA (JOSH HUTCHERSON), MARVEL (JACK QUAID), CATO (ALEXANDER LUDWIG), AND ALLAN POPPLETON, THE CO-STUNT COORDINATOR

Lawrence grins, describing her regimen. "I did every kind of training you can possibly imagine for this role. I had a running coach and I did stunt training so, you know, I did wall climbs and vaults and jumps and all sorts of stuff. I had archery for many weeks . . . it was rough, but it was fun. Archery is such a mind game. You have to just focus on one thing and if you get it wrong you get whipped with a string going over a hundred miles an hour. And it is painful, believe me." Before filming began, she was driving some fifty or sixty miles around Los Angeles every day, from stunt training to wardrobe fitting to archery practice, getting in shape for the movie.

Once her physical training was over, there was still more. Lawrence admiringly recalls working with T-Bone Burnett, the twelve-time Grammy Award winning musician who has worked on movies such as *Crazy Heart* and *O Brother, Where Art Thou?* "T-Bone Burnett is producing the music, which is still unbelievable to me. So he trained me a little bit with the singing. I have the worst voice in the world, so that was probably one of the hardest things he's had

to do, but I sang the melody, the lullaby, in my big scene with Rue."

Josh Hutcherson remembers, "Everyone else was learning how to do the weapons and things like that. And in this film, Peeta doesn't do a whole lot with the weapons. So for me it was all about getting to the right physical condition, which was bigger than I was. They wanted me to put on about fifteen pounds of pure muscle for the role, so I had to eat a lot of food and I was working out five days a week — it was very rigorous."

Liam Hemsworth had the opposite challenge. "I'm not in the Games, so I didn't have to do any fight training. But it was more just not eating as much as what I was eating. I wanted to look hungry."

The Hunger Games book became the actors' guide to the interior life of the characters they were about to play. Jennifer Lawrence recalls, "After I got the part, I read the first book over and over. It's great when you have a movie based on a book, because you can read the inner monologue of the character and that's incredibly helpful."

GARY ROSS GIVES FEEDBACK TO
JENNIFER LAWRENCE (KATNISS) AND
LIAM HEMSWORTH (GALE) WHILE
WORKING ON THE DISTRICT 12 SCENES.

FROM LEFT TO RIGHT: CLOVE (ISABELLE FUHRMAN), CATO (ALEXANDER LUDWIG), THRESH (DAYO OKENIYI), RUE (AMANDLA STENBERG)

The actors playing the tributes had some further exploration to do. Gary Ross was instrumental in asking probing questions to figure out who these characters really were.

For instance, Jack Quaid came to understand Marvel like this: "I'd say if he were in high school, he would be good at one thing and one thing only, and he'd let academics and everything else kind of slide. He is totally vicious. He doesn't care what he's cutting up — he just goes for it."

Alexander Ludwig began to see his character, Cato, as somebody even more brutal. "I like to think that Cato, before he gets into the Games, is kind of popular and charming, but he's always had that violent anger inside of him. When he gets into the Games he gets lost in this whole sick game and he almost goes insane toward the end."

Amandla Stenberg says, "My character's fighting style is to evade, because she knows that she can't fight the big, tough guys. She knows that if she tries, she'll lose. So what she does is she climbs in the trees and she eats eggs from birds, and that's her style — to outlast everyone else."

And Dayo Okeniyi, who portrays Thresh, came to see his character as a sort of gentle giant. "There's not too much of a backstory for my character, so that was great, because I got the chance to make it up. He's very family-oriented and he'll do anything to make it back to District Eleven to see his mom and his brother again. Thresh is a large character, and a presence to be reckoned with. But he doesn't want to get in anybody's way; he's not out for blood. He just wants to survive."

The tributes, also, were changing their looks and sharpening their skills.

Dayo Okeniyi says, "I was put on a rigorous diet of just protein, and a lot of chicken, a lot of vegetables, because I had to gain weight but I had to gain good weight."

Jack Quaid also had to bulk up for his role. "They got me a personal trainer and I put on about sixteen pounds of muscle. It's good to do something you love for a living and then, at the same time, get in the best shape you've ever been in. That's just nice."

Meanwhile, stunt coordinators Allan Poppleton and Chad Stahelski were preparing to teach the tributes the fight skills their characters would need to know for the scenes in the Training Center and in the arena. They'd had about eight weeks to put the sequences together, and were eager to see them in action.

Jon Kilik notes, "Safety in a movie like this was a

paramount concern for us. With all the stunts, action, fights and weapons, the welfare of the actors and crew was a big priority. Some of those swords and daggers are real, and we constantly had to be aware of the dangers."

Before teaching the cast each sequence, Stahelski and Poppleton tried to have a few days alone with the stunt performers. That way, when everyone trained together, some of the group was already familiar with the choreography.

Chad Stahelski says, "We took them into the gym and kind of had *Romper Room*. We trained them to do certain things and to get certain performances out of them. Everybody was game to do everything, but some of the exercises were done with

> "IT'S GOOD TO DO SOMETHING
> YOU LOVE FOR A LIVING AND
> THEN, AT THE SAME TIME, GET
> IN THE BEST SHAPE YOU'VE
> EVER BEEN IN. THAT'S JUST
> NICE."

stunt tributes only, for time restraints and, of course, for safety reasons."

"We did some very intense fight training. That's what I was focusing on the most, because that is

what Cato is, really," says Alexander Ludwig. "Cato's weapon of choice is a giant steel sword. I like to think I've become very skilled with the sword. . . ."

Isabelle Fuhrman, who plays Clove, adds, "I will say I do know how to throw a knife properly now, which is kind of creepy and a skill that I probably won't use, but it's just fun to say, you know? 'What'd you learn this summer?' 'Oh, I learned how to throw knives.' Just casually."

To prepare for the fight sequences, the stunt coordinators looked to the actors themselves. "It's not like we took any of the tributes and started training them in karate or kickboxing or jujitsu or anything like that," Stahelski points out. "We just took Isabelle or we took Zander [Alexander Ludwig] or we took any of the other ones and found out what they were good at, what character they had. We just kind of took that and ran with it during the big fight sequences, like at the Cornucopia. When you see the struggles between them on film, they're wild and emotional — they feel like kids fighting on the playground. That's the concept Gary wanted, and we took that to the next level when we added the weapons."

All of these preparations were about to come together with the vision of the design team to create one unforgettable film.

PART 3

THE LOOK OF *THE HUNGER GAMES:* PLACES AND PROPS

Early in the process of making a movie, the director works with his or her design team to formulate the film's look. For *The Hunger Games*, there would need to be *many* looks to capture the spectrum of life in Panem. There would be the look of the districts first, and later the look of the Capitol — it would be essential to set them apart from one another, to underscore the injustices that Collins had set up in her novel. On top of that, there would be the look of the arena itself. It would be a formidable challenge for Gary Ross to make these different pieces appear to be part of one whole.

Phil Messina, production designer for movies in the *Ocean's Eleven* series, as well as many others, explains his role like this: "I design the physical environment that the actors act in. I select locations and design a lot of the virtual environment, too." Before sets were built or costumes were designed, Messina was working with Ross to set the overall tone.

Messina first encountered *The Hunger Games* when Gary Ross urged him to read the book. Messina remembers: "Gary said, 'Read the book and tell me what you think.' He texted me probably three or four times when I was reading. 'You done yet? What part are you on?' And it was great — I literally read it overnight. Visually, it was striking."

Messina and Ross began to conceive what the different places in the movie would look like, from the Seam to the Capitol to the arena. They found photos that might guide these looks, and presented their ideas to Lionsgate.

"We went with sort of an Appalachian coal-mining vibe for the Seam," says Messina. "But then we added little bits and pieces, things that would have survived through the decades. We were careful not to make it feel like they were living in the Depression era — there was an allusion to that, but we added more modern elements, too," like appliances and outdated cars.

KATNISS WALKS ALONG THE FENCE
THAT SURROUNDS DISTRICT 12.

TOP: AN EARLY DIGITAL RENDERING OF WHAT A STREET IN DISTRICT 12 MIGHT LOOK LIKE. BOTTOM: AN ARTIST'S DIGITAL RENDERING OF MINERS IN DISTRICT 12.

He continues: "There wasn't a very specific description of the Capitol in the book. As I was doing research, I found these buildings from the World's Fair in New York, when General Motors built a giant complex. And it just seemed to vibe with what we had been talking about, so we riffed off of that for the Capitol. The buildings are pure advertisements of industry. They have a scalelessness, like you can't tell if they're ten feet tall or a thousand feet tall."

Director Ross was thinking the same way. "It was important to me that the Capitol evoke a sense of power and might and authority. Well, that's not spires going up to the sky — that's too fanciful. That's light. So we started to see the Capitol's power reflected in vast horizontal open space punctuated by buildings that are incredibly solid, heavy in mass."

What the images had in common were deep American roots: Some were from the American past, and some were past American ideas of what the future might look like. The American references made great sense to Nina Jacobson, who points out, "You don't want the audience to be let off the hook in this movie. This is us in the future, if we're not careful." Once this base was established, everything else grew out of it.

The next step was to decide where to do the filming.

What comes to mind when you think of North Carolina? Lush forests, perhaps. Mist rising over the Great Smoky Mountains. An All-American road trip down the Blue Ridge Parkway. The haunting sound of a banjo. It's not the first place you'd think to locate an arena where two dozen teenagers fight to the death, or a city full of foolish spectators who cannot look away. Yet Gary Ross saw its possibilities from the beginning. A state with thousands of acres of forests — but also a modern city, Charlotte — might manage to serve his multiple needs.

"What we've been able to do," Messina explains, "is use a lot of actual locations and amend them and bring them into the world of the movie, so it's not all created from the ground up." In other

> "IT WAS IMPORTANT TO ME THAT THE CAPITOL EVOKE A SENSE OF POWER AND MIGHT AND AUTHORITY."

words, Ross and Messina tackled two tasks simultaneously: scouting locations and building sets in North Carolina.

For the Seam in District 12, they had an incredible stroke of luck. Messina says, "Through the North Carolina Film Commission, we ended up

The actual exterior of the
Everdeen house and other
dwellings in the Seam.

finding an abandoned mill town. There were thirty-five almost identical factory homes for the workers — they lived on the premises, right where they worked — it was absolutely perfect."

It appealed to Gary Ross because, as he puts it, "It's one thing to live in squalor, but it's another thing to live in squalor without any individuality, where the houses are cookie-cutter and manufactured by the company, not the people."

Messina's team built an interior in one of the houses — for the Everdeen family — and added details to the others to make it appear as if people were

> "WE BROUGHT IN ABOUT THREE HUNDRED FEET OF RAILROAD TRACK AND HAD TRAINS CRANED ONTO IT, PAINTED WITH *CAPITOL COAL.* WE TRIED TO EMPHASIZE THE IDEA THAT THE DISTRICT DIDN'T GET TO KEEP ITS RAW MATERIAL, THAT IT WAS GOING TO THE CAPITOL."
> — PHIL MESSINA

living in them. The only problem, really, was that Messina had first seen the town in winter, months before the filming began. "Without leaves and brown grass, it looked the right sort of dismal," he remembers. "As spring took hold, though, it started getting greener and more lush. It looked sort of like a golf course." Before the cast arrived, the crew plucked leaves off trees and covered patches of grass so it would turn brown.

In Shelby, North Carolina, Messina's location manager, Todd Christensen, found an old warehouse complex where the people of District 12 might gather for the reaping. "Phil wanted a big enough square to do our scenes, which meant we had to cut one of the buildings in half," he remembers. "I had to negotiate

AN ARENA TREE BUILT BY THE
PRODUCTION DESIGN TEAM.

that. And then the building was filled with junk, so we had to find the guy who owned it to get the junk out — so we could cut the building in half. It's one of those things that people don't know about that happens in order to make a look."

On one of the warehouse walls the team built a Hall of Justice, the Capitol's headquarters in the district. And the Capitol's shadow was also visible in the railroad cars Messina had painted with *Capitol Coal* and lowered onto the site with cranes. Just to emphasize, says Messina, "that the district's raw material was not going to them — it was going to the Capitol."

Near Charlotte, a former Philip Morris plant was sitting empty. Todd Christensen says, "When I got here in February they were toward the end of cutting up every piece of machinery for scrap and they had cleared out this building in order to sell it." It was a two-thousand-acre campus, with three million square feet of manufacturing and office space.

Messina and Ross had talked about building a Training Center for the tributes, but because it was

in the Capitol it would have to be enormous. "I suggested to Gary that he come and look at this Philip Morris plant because there were some huge spaces." It had high ceilings, no pillars, and just the scale the production needed. Rather than build a Training Center from scratch, the team decided to construct one within the plant. There was plenty of room to create multiple training stations for the tributes, as well as a balcony for the Gamemakers.

Even the woods locations required a great deal of advance planning. Messina scouted in various state parks in January and February. "I was scouting in the snow, with no leaves on any of the trees. I'm referring back to books about what this place looks like in the summertime and there's a little bit of a leap of faith, but ultimately it worked out well."

Ross adds, "The arena's obviously in the forest and I wanted it to be different from a lot of forests you see in movies. I wanted it to have hardwoods — I didn't want it to be just coniferous. I wanted it to feel uniquely American."

Eventually they used the same woods for District 12 and the arena, but postproduction work changed the lighting and the feel of the arena setting, so the

A MODEL OF THE AVENUE OF THE TRIBUTES.

THREE LOCATIONS IN THE CAPITOL. TOP LEFT: A FILM STILL OF THE CONTROL ROOM. TOP RIGHT: CONCEPT ART FOR THE COUNTDOWN TO THE HUNGER GAMES. BOTTOM: CONCEPT ART FOR THE CAPITOL TRAIN STATION.

PEETA AND KATNISS IN THE LIVING ROOM
OF THE TRAINING CENTER APARTMENT.

LAWRENCE AND HUTCHERSON
BEGIN A SCENE IN THE ARENA.

woods didn't look quite natural, but more like a creation of the Gamemakers. As Messina describes it, "We just took out a little bit of the haphazardness of nature."

Creating the Cornucopia was a special challenge to the design team. "In the book it says that it's a cornucopia like the one that's used at holiday time," says director Gary Ross. "But we paused and wondered: What does that mean in the future? I wanted to create a large metallic sculptural element that almost seemed like a knife-edge into the natural world. We came up with this faceted, sculptural object that felt evocative of the Capitol: hard and cold."

Messina explains, "We looked at some of Frank Gehry's work such as Disney Hall and we looked at a lot of modern architecture that's taking place right now, with sort of folded planes. I think Suzanne

> "THE BIGGEST DESIGN CHALLENGE IN THIS MOVIE IS THAT THE HUNGER GAMES TAKE PLACE IN THE WOODS. SO YOU HAVE TO FIND THE RIGHT WOODS, YOU HAVE TO FIND BEAUTIFUL PLACES, YOU HAVE TO FIND PLACES THAT HAVE THE RIGHT GEOGRAPHY FOR THE GAMES."
> — ROBIN BISSELL

described it as being painted gold, but we ended up going with a gunmetal gray. It's actually one of my favorite pieces in the movie. We built it in Charlotte and trucked it out to Asheville, set it out with a crane on location."

Set decorator Larry Dias was responsible for furniture, lighting, carpets — anything not a floor or a wall on a location or a set. "I go into an empty

THE CREW CONSTRUCTS THE CORNUCOPIA.

KATNISS BARTERS IN THE HOB.

shell of the set and then put everything inside of it," he explains. Once Ross and Messina had articulated their overall vision, and identified or created places for filming, Dias could get to work.

At first he thought it could be difficult to decorate the Everdeens' house. The location was perfect, but where would he find the furniture to flesh it out? "I'd never worked in North Carolina," he says. "I wasn't really sure what I was going to be able to acquire here, so we'd done a lot of prep work in Los Angeles. But once I got here I realized, it's kind of a treasure trove for this type of a movie. The first day I got to North Carolina, Sara Gardner-Gail, my assistant, and I did a little research, trying to find some antique stores. And we happened to find one that's literally less than a mile from the Philip Morris plant where we're shooting — eighty-eight thousand square feet of antiques. We hit the mother lode on day one." They bought

tables, chairs, photographs, all in keeping with the visual tone of the film.

Even with such a rich source of materials, Dias had a harder time finding stuff to fill the Hob. He says, "The Hob was difficult because you're trying to create a marketplace with things that have no value except to the people that live within the Seam." Luckily, he found a man who was "sort of an antiques dealer, but his antiques are in an unfinished, raw state. He has a yard, probably on forty acres, so there's a lot of stuff outside that's just in piles and heaps. We were able to get lots of stuff there."

When it came time to decorate the town square, Dias says, "We sourced these giant glass balls that became the reaping balls and rigged them onto some tables that we found here in North Carolina. We outfitted them to make them look like they were a tool of the Capitol, sent out to all the districts. So

EFFIE TRINKET (ELIZABETH
BANKS) PICKS A NAME
FROM THE REAPING BALL.

TOP: THE REMAKE CENTER IN THE CAPITOL.
BOTTOM: THE DRESSING ROOM OF THE
AMPHITHEATER WHERE KATNISS PREPARES FOR
HER INTERVIEW WITH CAESAR FLICKERMAN.

THE TRIBUTES IN THE HOVERCRAFT
THAT WILL BRING THEM TO THE ARENA.
RUE AND CLOVE SIT IN THE SEATS
CLOSEST TO THE CAMERA.

all the districts, when we see the reapings, have the same balls."

Just as Messina had looked to the past to design the Capitol's exteriors, Dias looked to the past to create its interiors. In addition, he says, "There's a coldness to it all, a sort of spare quality. The spaces lack anything personal." He special-ordered period pieces from the 1960s and 1970s, and mixed this furniture with light fixtures from a North Carolina showroom.

The Capitol's style extended even to the interior of the hovercraft, which Dias helped to design. "Inside the hovercraft, we were going after a militaristic feel. There's a coldness to it, too, obviously. They're taking these kids off to these Games, and they all know what's going to happen next. I found the seats early on — they're actually NASCAR race-car seats. I found a North Carolina manufacturer less than a mile away, and we customized the seats.

Made them all have symmetry instead of asymmetry, because that's what the Capitol would have."

Trish Gallaher Glenn, the movie's prop master, was responsible for everything the actors picked up and touched in the movie. One of her greatest challenges was making sure that Katniss's weapons were representative of the various places she used them.

"Katniss has two bows in the movie," says Glenn. "The first bow is the hunting bow that her father has made, that she hides in the district. We wanted something very organic, very real, very simple. And we wanted the other bow for the Games to reflect the Capitol, as if everything that was made for the Games was made by artisans in the Capitol. We went black and silver, and we tried to do a lot of combinations of matte and shiny. And we wanted super-clean lines. Her arrows for the Games are bright and shiny, silver aluminum rods with a really elongated tip. We did the fletching, which would

AN EARLY DIGITAL RENDERING OF THE HOVERCRAFT THAT
BRINGS THE TRIBUTES TO THE ARENA.

be the feathers on the arrow, in a clear plastic with silver Mylar on it. And we had Jennifer pull them, we had her run with them, so that we could all see and make sure we had it right."

Glenn also created the other tributes' weapons, which had to look lethal but be practical during filming. She says, "Some weapons are made of aluminum. It's a super-high-quality aluminum that you can actually fight with, blade on blade, metal on metal. Then we figure out if we need any rubber replicas, soft ones you can hit somebody over the head with."

A CLOSE-UP OF THE BACKPACK KATNISS GRABS AT THE START OF THE GAMES — WITH A KNIFE PROTRUDING.

Careful thought went into designing the parachutes that deliver sponsors' gifts to the tributes during the Hunger Games. Glenn says, "When I read the book, it said 'a tiny parachute' and somehow in my mind it was something very, very small. But when you get the reality that Katniss gets a roll, she gets soup, she gets all these different medicines in the parachute and the container is beneath the parachute . . . it had to expand a lot. We kind of went into this direction that it's all being controlled anyway by the Capitol, that

it didn't really have to be working but it should appear to be controllable."

The Capitol's cruelty even extended to the shocking color of the berries Glenn chose. "We started out thinking, well, maybe we can take blueberries, those really big blueberries that you can find at a certain time of year, and dye them," she says. "And that didn't work at all. So we came up with a wild berry that I ordered online, and this particular one that I think is pretty amazing. The juice of it is red, bright red, almost like blood, which we thought was really cool. We went with a frozen one and we have this technique for defrosting them very slowly with paper towels, and we try to keep them as dry as possible so they don't squish. Still, they were everywhere. Scott Hankins, the costumer, hated us for a few days because of the berry juice that was all over the costumes."

Gary Ross and Phil Messina hired Jack White, a food stylist, to design and create the food of Panem. "When we were at District Twelve, there were a few scenes with Katniss and her mom where her mom is cooking. The beans and the greens that we had for them to eat looked almost rotten. The thought was not to bring in beautiful food, but to pick stuff that looked almost like it was about to decompose."

In the Capitol, though, he worked with fresh food and bright colors. "Blues, oranges, greens . . . but not any pastels, not any earth tones. Nothing brown." White's job was not to make food that the actors would eat while filming, but rather to make food that seemed right for the strange and luxurious world of the Capitol. "I have to make things that could last twelve hours on the set. Showpieces, really. Israeli couscous — you can make that any color you want. And quail eggs. Two seconds in a colored water and they come out looking beautiful."

Food plays an unusually important role in *The Hunger Games*, since it's one way the Capitol

TOP: PHIL MESSINA, PRODUCTION DESIGNER, ARRANGES THE FOOD IN THE TRAIN CAR.
BELOW: EXAMPLES OF CAPITOL FOOD.

exerts its power over the districts. People feast in the Capitol while they starve in the districts, and over the course of the book Katniss's experiences are reflected in the food she eats. "Before the Games, when Katniss is at home, she's hungry," says Jack White. "She's having to hunt for food, struggling to find something to eat. Then, as she's on her way to the Games, she experiences — for the first time — an abundance of food. It's probably the first time in her life that she's seen that much, and it's all available to her. Then, once she arrives in the Capitol, it's completely over the top and she's not even sure what it is that she's getting to see."

As Collins lavished attention on the food in her book, Ross lavished attention on the smallest food details in the film, working with Jack White to bring his vision to life.

Creating the bread of District 11, for instance, was a long process. White remembers, "In the movie, Katniss receives a gift from District Eleven — the roll floats down to her in the arena. The director was very specific in what he wanted that roll to look like. So I think we made about fifteen or twenty different kinds of rolls. They all had to be a specific size and weight to make sure they would fit in the container. It ended up being a half-wheat, half-white flour, so that gave it a nice color. We were stenciling the number *11* on, until the director asked us if we could try to burn it in. So then that involved another company that did the brands for us. We had to find the right font for that. Then they decided they'd like to see a ring around the number, so that was another step. I had the eleven burned right into the center of the roll, but that looked too perfect — it needed to seem more like an afterthought, so the brand ended up in the right-hand corner. And then I had to make seventy-five of those, because you can't just have one."

Likewise, a great deal of thought and effort went into creating the bread that Peeta throws

Katniss when she's on the brink of starvation. White says, "We went to a bakery in Asheville and we got several samples of different sizes of bread to show Gary, and Gary picked the one he liked. In the scene, Peeta throws burned bread from his family's bakery to Katniss. So we stood with a blowtorch and burned roll after roll. They used two per take, and it was raining in the scene, so we needed a lot of extras."

White worked closely with other members of the design team to make sure that the food created a flawless look together with the sets and the props. "Some of the food choices depend on what the set decorator, Larry Dias, does. For instance I need to know what the plates look like before

> **"WE STOOD WITH A BLOWTORCH AND BURNED ROLL AFTER ROLL. THEY USED TWO PER TAKE, AND IT WAS RAINING IN THE SCENE, SO WE NEEDED A LOT OF EXTRAS."**

I know what sort of food I can put on them. On one of my first jobs, they ordered lobster for the scenes, and the lobster was three times bigger than the plate."

And when he cooked for the filming, he always cooked extra, in case something went wrong. "The suckling pig was cooked with something in its mouth to keep it open. After it was cooked, we replaced that with an apple. We had to make three pigs because if something happened while they were shooting the arrow into the apple, we'd be up the creek. Every take, we put a new apple in there."

The visual sense of the movie began with the locations and props, but soon extended to the characters at the heart of the story.

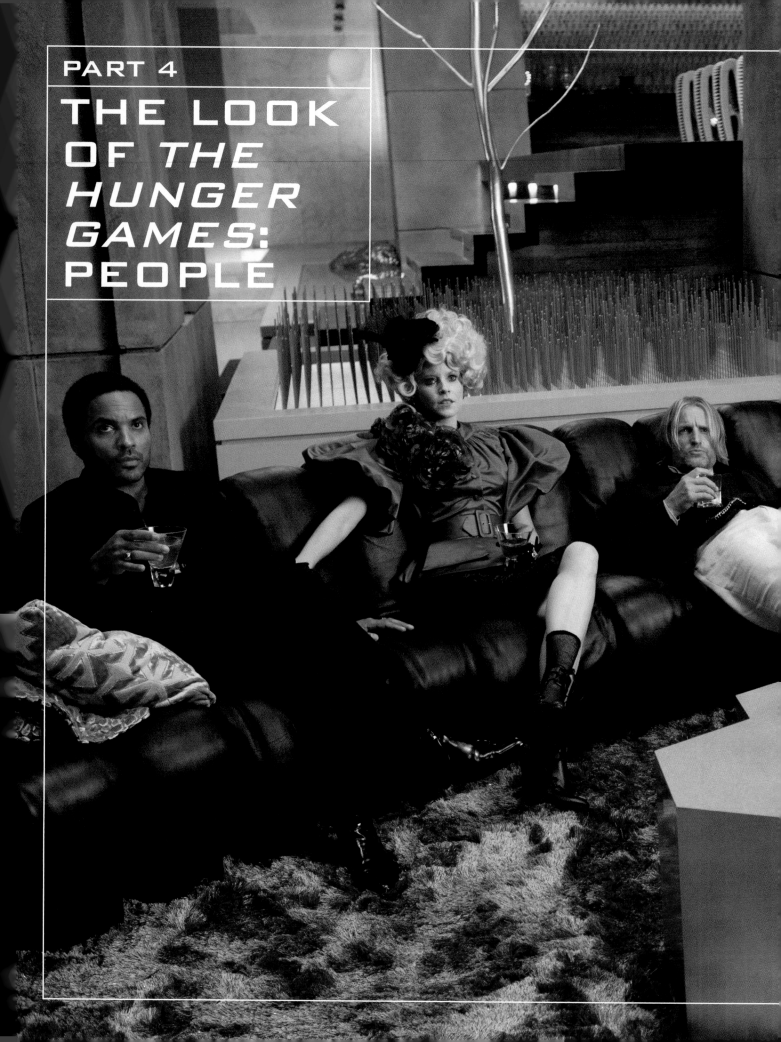

PART 4

THE LOOK OF *THE HUNGER GAMES:* PEOPLE

ow that the overall look of the movie was in place, it was time to design the look of the characters. Costume designer Judianna Makovsky spoke extensively with Gary Ross early on about a general look for the characters in *The Hunger Games*. "Gary and I agreed that it had to be a recognizable world, not a foreign, futuristic world," Makovsky says. "People needed to be able to relate to it." She smiles and adds, "But it was really fun for us, too. We could do outrageous things that we don't usually get to do in a movie."

Makovsky worked with makeup artist Ve Neill and hair department head Linda Flowers. Between them, the three had designed costumes, hair, and makeup for dozens of movies and garnered three Academy Awards® and eleven Academy Award® nominations. "The way I work as a designer, I don't just design a frock," Makovsky says. "I'm designing a person. I start from the head and go to the foot. I work very closely with makeup and hair and we design it all together. I have the most collaborative team and I think it's more successful that way."

ABOVE: ROWS OF WIGS FOR THE CAPITOL CAST MEMBERS. RIGHT: THE HEADDRESSES FOR THE TRIBUTES TO WEAR IN THE TRIBUTE PARADE.

THE LOOK OF *THE HUNGER GAMES*: PEOPLE

"THE DISTRICTS WERE GOING TO BE A VERY LIMITED PALETTE. SINCE DISTRICT TWELVE IS FOR MINING, WE DECIDED TO GO WITH A LOT OF GRAY. NOT LIKE A SEPIA-TONED FILM, THOUGH — A SORT OF BLUE-GRAY."

—JUDIANNA MAKOVSKY

BAKERY
·FRESH BREAD
BISCU

"I'D NEVER SEEN JENNIFER WITH DARK HAIR, AND SHE IS
SO STUNNING WITH DARK HAIR. FOR HER MAKEUP, WHEN
WE STARTED OFF IN DISTRICT TWELVE, WE WANTED TO
KEEP HER AS NATURAL AS POSSIBLE. BEAUTIFUL AND
UNAFFECTED."
— VE NEILL

"IN DISTRICT TWELVE, THE WOMEN ARE SIMPLY BRAIDED,
HAIR PULLED BACK OUT OF THE WAY, OR JUST SIMPLY
CUT OFF SO THEY DON'T HAVE TO DEAL WITH THE HEAT
AND THE LENGTH."
— LINDA FLOWERS

"SINCE YOU SEE GALE SO LITTLE IN THE FILM, WE JUST WANTED TO KEEP HIM REALLY HANDSOME, WHICH IS NOT HARD TO DO. HIS CLOTHES ARE OLD, THERE'S NOTHING NEW. HE'S VERY POOR, SO HE DOESN'T HAVE A LOT OF CLOTHES.

"WE DID GO WITH THAT DESCRIPTION IN THE BOOK THAT KATNISS WEARS A BLUE DRESS TO THE REAPING, AND IT HAS A VERY VINTAGE FEEL, THAT DRESS. WE FOUND VINTAGE FABRIC THAT WE DYED TO THE PERFECT COLOR. WE WANTED A SIMPLICITY, BUT AN ELEGANCE, TO THAT DRESS. IT'S SOMETHING THAT COULD HAVE BEEN HER MOTHER'S."
— JUDIANNA MAKOVSKY

"IT WAS IN MY DISCUSSIONS WITH GARY AND WOODY THAT HAYMITCH EVOLVED INTO A LITTLE BIT OF A FOP."
— JUDIANNA MAKOVSKY

"FOR HAYMITCH'S HAIR, WE MADE IT LIKE A DISTRICT TWELVE LOOK, ALL GROWN OUT. LIKE HE'S JUST NOT MAINTAINING HIMSELF ANY-MORE. IT'S SCRAGGLY AND LONGER AND A LITTLE SAD."
— LINDA FLOWERS

"JOSH WALKED IN WITH DARK HAIR AND WE HAD TO BLEACH IT OUT A COUPLE OF TIMES AND COLOR IT. TO LOOK AT HIM NOW, IT LOOKS SO NATURAL ON HIM, BUT WHEN HE CAME IN I WONDERED IF WE COULD MAKE SOMEONE THAT DARK INTO A NATURAL-LOOKING BLOND. BUT I THINK BLEACHING THE EYEBROWS AND DOING DIFFERENT TONES OF BLONDS IN HIS HAIR REALLY WORKED. I MEAN, LIKE, JOSH IS PEETA. HE'S EVERYTHING PEETA IS. HE JUST DOESN'T HAVE PEETA'S BLOND HAIR, SO WE GAVE IT TO HIM. I CAN GIVE THEM HAIR, YOU KNOW, BUT I CAN'T GIVE THEM THAT WHOLE PRESENCE THAT'S JUST PER-FECT FOR THE CHARACTER."
— LINDA FLOWERS

"I'D WORKED WITH ELIZA-BETH BANKS BEFORE, AND WE HAD A GREAT RAPPORT. AND WE DECIDED EFFIE'S A LITTLE PRIM, BUT OUTRA-GEOUS. WHEN SHE'S IN DIS-TRICT TWELVE, SHE TONES IT DOWN A LITTLE BIT, AND WHEN SHE GETS TO THE CAPITOL IT GETS A LITTLE CRAZIER. SHE CHANGES WIGS WITH EVERY OUTFIT."

— JUDIANNA MAKOVSKY

"YOU HAVE THIS COMPLETELY DEPRESSED AREA, AND THEN YOU HAVE EFFIE, WHO COMES FROM THIS OPULENT CAPI-TOL. WHEN SHE SHOWS UP, SHE IS VERY SHOCKING COM-PARED TO WHAT YOU HAVE BEEN SEEING. AND THAT'S HER SUBDUED LOOK! SHE'S A VISUAL BRIDGE BETWEEN DISTRICT TWELVE AND THE CAPITOL."

— VE NEILL

"WHEN YOU GET TO THE CAPITOL, WELL, WE HAVE TWO PALETTES. ONE IS A VERY BRIGHT PASTEL, A LOT OF FUCHSIA AND TURQUOISE AND PINK. BUT WE ALSO LIKE THE PAINTINGS OF MAX BECKMANN, SO THERE'S A LOT OF HIDEOUS ACID YELLOWS AND GREENS. PLUS A LOT OF BLACK TO MUTE THE BRIGHTNESS OF THE OUTRAGEOUS COLORS."
— JUDIANNA MAKOVSKY

"WHEN YOU START DOING THESE BRIGHT LOOKS AND COLORS, YOU'RE WORRIED THAT IT'S GONNA COME ACROSS LIKE A HALLOWEEN PARTY OR CARNIVAL, AND THIS IS A VERY ADVANCED, SMART SOCIETY. SO THERE'S A FINE LINE OF CREATING A LOOK THAT WOULD BE ACCEPTABLE FOR THAT TYPE OF CHARACTER AND IT DOESN'T LOOK TOO WHIMSICAL, TOO FUN. BECAUSE THE CAPITOL ISN'T FUN."
— LINDA FLOWERS

"WE DECIDED TO KEEP LENNY KRAVITZ MOSTLY IN BLACK, NOT FRILLS LIKE EVERYBODY ELSE. NO COLOR IN THE HAIR. HE HAS GOLD EYELINER, AND I DON'T THINK YOU NEED TO DO MUCH MORE THAN THAT."
— JUDIANNA MAKOVSKY

"FOR KATNISS WE STAYED WITH HER SIGNATURE BRAID LIKE THE BOOK, BUT I TRIED TO MAKE IT AN INTEREST-ING BRAID. HAVING TO TAKE SOMETHING AS SIMPLE AS A BRAID AND MAKE IT LOOK IN-TERESTING, LIKE SOMETHING THAT SOMEONE MIGHT WEAR IN THE FUTURE — EVEN NOW — IS A CHALLENGE."

— LINDA FLOWERS

"THE GIRL-ON-FIRE DRESS — IT'S A VERY SIMPLE DRESS, BUT IT HAS THESE INSERTS THAT HAVE SWAROVSKI CRYSTALS ON THE INSIDE SO THE DRESS REALLY SPARKLES WHEN SHE TWIRLS. THERE'S A WHOLE UNDERLAYER THAT'S MADE OF OTHER THINGS, SO YOU JUST GET GLIMPSES OF THAT WHEN SHE TWIRLS. BUT WHEN SHE'S JUST STANDING, IT'S A BEAUTIFUL DRESS WITH AN INTERESTING PLEATED BOTTOM."

— JUDIANNA MAKOVSKY

"THEN, WHEN SHE GETS INTO HER INTERVIEWS, THAT WAS REALLY FUN. I HAD ORDERED THESE FABULOUS EYELASHES FROM LONDON AND THEY'RE MADE OUT OF PAPER. THE ONES I USED ON HER ARE LIKE LITTLE PEACOCKS. THROUGH THE FEATHERS I PAINTED A FLASH OF TURQUOISE. I DID THE SAME LOOK WITH HER FOUNDATION, AND ONE MORE SPECIAL THING . . . OFF THE SHOULDER OF HER DRESS, I DID A FLAME EFFECT THAT HAD SWAROVSKI STONES IN IT. IT LOOKS LIKE IT JUST EXPLODED OFF INTO HER SKIN. I GAVE HER SOFT, BEAUTIFUL, FROSTED ARMS — SHE WAS REALLY EXCITED, LIKE A PRINCESS THAT DAY."

— VE NEILL

"IN THE BOOK, EVERY TRIB-
UTE WEARS EXACTLY THE
SAME THING TO THE GAMES.
THEY'RE ALL ON AN EQUAL
BASIS. THAT'S FINE IN A
BOOK. BUT IN A FILM, YOU'RE
NOT GOING TO KNOW WHO
ANYBODY IS IF EVERYBODY'S
IN A BLACK JACKET. SO GARY
MADE THE DECISION THAT
EACH DISTRICT WOULD HAVE
THEIR OWN COLOR JACKET
AND EVERYTHING ELSE COULD
BE THE SAME.

"WE WANTED THINGS THAT
WOULD BLEND IN WITH THE
FOREST AND WE NEEDED
SOMETHING THAT LOOKED A
LITTLE HIGH-TECH. WE ALSO
WANTED VERY LIGHTWEIGHT
GARMENTS, THINGS THAT
WOULD PICK UP THE LIGHT
AT NIGHT. SO WE MADE THE
DECISION TO DO A JACKET
THAT HAD THIS OUTER LAYER
OF PARACHUTE NYLON."
— JUDIANNA MAKOVSKY

"CLOVE IS KIND OF A MEAN GIRL, YOU KNOW; SHE LIKES TO THROW KNIVES AND SHE'S PRETTY BRUTAL. I THINK I WAS INSPIRED BY THOSE OLD JAPANESE KUNG FU MOVIES WHERE YOU SEE THOSE WOMEN WITH THEIR PONYTAILS, WITH KNIVES IN THEM. SO WE GAVE HER A PONYTAIL ON TOP OF HER HEAD, BUT TO MAKE IT DIFFERENT WE MADE IT LOOK LIKE LITTLE BALLS COMING DOWN OFF HER HEAD.

"AND THEN THERE'S GLIMMER, WHO'S THE PRETTY ONE, SO WE KEPT HER GLAMOROUS. WE DID SOME FISHBONE BRAIDING IN HER HAIR. OF COURSE, WE HAD TO REMEMBER THAT THESE GIRLS ARE GONNA GO FIGHT, SO THEY'RE NOT GONNA BE ALL DOWN LIKE THEY'RE PRETTY. THEY'RE SERIOUS."
— LINDA FLOWERS

"ONE OF THE DECISIONS WE MADE REGARDING PEETA BEFORE THE GAMES WAS NOT TO SHOW HOW MUSCULAR HE IS, NOT TO GIVE IT AWAY. IT'S A SURPRISE, LATER, WHEN WE SEE HIS STRENGTH."
—JUDIANNA MAKOVSKY

"IN THE BOOK, PEETA AND KATNISS WEAR EXACTLY THE SAME COSTUME FOR THE CHARIOT SCENE. BUT WE HAD TO CHANGE THINGS — ONE'S A BOY'S VERSION, ONE'S A GIRL'S VERSION. THEY'RE SIMILAR, BUT DIFFERENT. IN THE BOOK, IT'S BASICALLY A LEOTARD AND TIGHTS WITH SOME TALL BOOTS, AND WE DECIDED IT HAD TO HAVE THE LOOK AND SHINE OF COAL AND BE MORE DRAMATIC. OF COURSE THE FLAMES ARE MAGIC — CINNA DOES THE FLAMES. BUT WE TRIED TO KEEP THAT FEEL IN THE SHINE."

— JUDIANNA MAKOVSKY

"BASICALLY WHAT I'VE TRIED TO DO WITH [KATNISS], EVEN WITH HER BEAUTY MAKEUP AT THE CAPITOL, IS TO KEEP HER AS YOUTHFUL AS POSSIBLE. EVEN IN THE CHARIOT SCENE, THE AVENUE OF THE TRIBUTES CLOTHING. I JUST DID A LITTLE LASH ON THE OUTSIDE OF HER EYE, AND I PUT A LITTLE ORANGE FLICKER ON THE END, AND A BEAUTIFUL SOFT CHEEK. SHE HAD THIS REALLY FABULOUS PLAITED HAIR AND IT WAS ALMOST A ROMAN OR GREEK LOOK."

—VE NEILL

"WE DECIDED THAT CAESAR WAS A TYPICAL TV TALK SHOW HOST AND A LITTLE OUTRAGEOUS. SO WE KEPT THE BLUE SPARKLY SUIT THAT HE WEARS ON THE STAGE. WE WENT WITH THAT, BUT WE JUST TOOK IT A LITTLE BIT FURTHER. YOU DON'T HAVE TO GO TOO FAR WHEN YOU HAVE BLUE HAIR, FRANKLY. HIS CLOTHES ARE LIKE WHAT A TV HOST WOULD WEAR ON A BIG AWARDS SHOW."
— JUDIANNA MAKOVSKY

"STANLEY TUCCI HAD JUST COME OFF A VACATION SOMEPLACE WHERE HE GOT REALLY TAN. AND I THOUGHT HE COULD BE LIKE THE GEORGE HAMILTON OF THE CAPITOL — THAT'S KIND OF WHAT WE WENT FOR. HE WENT AND GOT HIS WIG ON AND HE WAS FABULOUS. WE DID HIS EYEBROWS A DARK BLUE TO COMPLEMENT THE WIG, AND THAT'S HOW WE CAME UP WITH CAESAR FLICKERMAN."
— VE NEILL

"DONALD SUTHERLAND IS A VERY ELEGANT MAN AND OF COURSE WE'RE GOING TO GO WITH HIS ELEGANCE. WE WANTED HIM TO BE IMPOSING, BUT WE DIDN'T WANT HIM TO LOOK LIKE THE REST OF THE CAPITOL, WITH OUTRAGEOUS FASHIONS. WE THOUGHT . . . HE'S ABOVE ALL THAT. HE CAN DO WHATEVER HE WANTS. BUT WE KEPT HIS HAIR LONG, LIKE HE'S A LION. A MAJESTIC LION."

— JUDIANNA MAKOVSKY

"I SAT AND WORKED WITH DONALD AN ENTIRE DAY. AND AFTER WE TRIED ALL OF THESE THINGS ON HIM, I SAID, 'WHAT IF WE JUST MAKE YOUR EYEBROWS ALL WHITE TO MATCH YOUR HAIR?' HE'S JOLLY-LOOKING, ALMOST LIKE SANTA CLAUS. HE LOOKS LIKE HE'S ALL WARM AND FUZZY WHEN IN FACT HE'S THE MOST EVIL OF THEM ALL."

— VE NEILL

"IN THE BOOK, THE GAMEMAKERS ALL WEAR LONG ROBES, BUT WE THOUGHT THAT WAS A LITTLE TOO SCIENCE-FICTIONY. WE WANTED SENECA — WES BENTLEY — IN A UNIFORM BECAUSE IT LOOKS MORE IMPOSING. AND HIS UNIQUE BEARD . . . THAT'S A CAPITOL LOOK."
—JUDIANNA MAKOVSKY

"I KEPT THINKING, YOU KNOW, WES HAS A GREAT BEARD. A NICE, HEAVY BEARD. I WANTED TO DO SOMETHING REALLY COOL WITH HIM. WHEN HE CAME IN, I PRECUT THE BEARD AND I KIND OF PENCILED IT ALL IN WITH SOME EYE SHADOW, BECAUSE I WASN'T SURE WHAT I WAS DOING. I TOOK PICTURES AND I JUST THOUGHT, WELL, I'LL SEND THESE TO GARY, SHOW HIM THE BASIC IDEA. GARY'S FIRST REACTION WAS 'MEPHISTOPHELES! IT'S LIKE HE'S THE DEVIL.' AND I THOUGHT, WELL, HE IS THE DEVIL. AND USUALLY BAD GUYS HAVE DARK EYES, BUT WES HAS THE HUGEST BLUE EYES I'VE EVER SEEN. SO TO HAVE THOSE PIERCING BLUE EYES AND THAT EVIL LOOK IS REALLY A FANTASTIC COMBINATION, I THINK."
—VE NEILL

"WHEN WE HAD FOUR
HUNDRED CAPITOL
EXTRAS, JUDIANNA AND
I OVERSAW THE ENTIRE
GROUP GETTING READY.
PEOPLE GOT SENT BACK
TWO AND THREE TIMES
BECAUSE THEY NEEDED
TO BE PERFECT. AND
NOT JUST FIFTY OR A
HUNDRED OF THEM. ALL
OF THEM HAD TO BE
PERFECT."
—VE NEILL

"WE ACTUALLY REDESIGNED A LOT OF THINGS WHEN WE REALIZED THAT WE WERE GOING TO BE SHOOTING IN NORTH CAROLINA IN AUGUST AND HAVE ALL OF THOSE WOMEN IN FURS. WE TRIED TO LIMIT WHERE WE PUT IT, HOW WE PUT IT ON THEM, SO THEY DON'T HAVE HEAT-STROKE."

—JUDIANNA MAKOVSKY

"I THINK WHAT WE WERE TRYING TO AVOID WAS THE SEVENTIES OR EIGHTIES KIND OF LOOK IN OUR CAPITOL SCENES. WE DIDN'T WANT ANY OF THAT TYPE OF EYE MAKEUP GOING ON. WE WANTED TO HAVE SOMETHING AVANT-GARDE — YOU KNOW, LIKE THINGS THAT YOU ONLY SEE IN MAGAZINES, THAT NOBODY WOULD EVER WEAR IN REAL LIFE. WE KIND OF TOOK THAT TO THE NEXT STEP. AND THEN WE BLEACHED EVERYBODY'S EYEBROWS, WHICH RIGHT IN ITSELF TAKES SOMEBODY TO A WHOLE OTHER LEVEL OF BIZARRENESS. EVEN THE MEN HAD COLORED HAIR. THEIR HAIR WAS SET. IT WAS JUST WILD AND FABULOUS, LIKE JEAN PAUL GAULTIER ON ACID. IT WAS REALLY FUN."

—VE NEILL

"WHEN WE WERE CREATING THE CAPITOL SCENES, WE HAD FOUR HUNDRED EXTRAS TO GET INTO MAKEUP. IT TOOK MY TEAM OF THIRTY PEOPLE NINE AND A HALF HOURS TO GET THE JOB DONE."
— VE NEILL

PART 5
THE FILMING OF
THE HUNGER GAMES

Shooting of *The Hunger Games* started on May 23, 2011, when director Gary Ross flew to North Carolina from Los Angeles. Many of the actors were assembled there already, with more to come as larger scenes were filmed. Locations had been identified, sets had been built. Training was finished, lines were memorized. Everything was ready to go.

Ross had a clear sense of the way he wanted to shoot the film, and it was different from any approach he'd taken in his previous movies. "One of the things that's most important here is to convey the immediacy, the first-person point of view that the book has. The cinematic style has to reflect that. So in this movie I got to shoot in a way that I'd never shot before — more urgent, more personal. I needed to give the audience that incredibly immediate sense that they're not watching this girl — they *are* this girl."

Wherever possible, then, he kept to Katniss's point of view. "I didn't want the audience to know more than the character knew. I wanted them to be in her shoes, to experience everything through her eyes," Ross adds. Occasionally the film cuts away to show developments in the Capitol that will affect Katniss, or reactions back home to her performance in the Games, but for most of the movie the audience is with Katniss, filled with suspense and fear.

Ross used a handheld camera to shoot some of the pivotal scenes, giving them an intense you-are-there feeling. Nina Jacobson explains, "It's a big movie, and at the same time we didn't want it to be

DIRECTOR GARY ROSS ON SET.

a grandiose movie. We wanted it to have a little bit of that guerrilla quality. It's set in the future, but it's not a movie that's all about technology."

While many of the young actors were new to filmmaking, they couldn't help but notice Ross's unusual technique. Dayo Okeniyi, who plays Thresh, says, "The fights are shot in a very gritty documentary-type style, almost like the Super Bowl. The camera gets right in there with us, and audiences are gonna feel like they are right there on the field, fighting for their lives."

The film was shot between May and September, beginning with some of the District 12 scenes, skipping ahead to most of the arena's action, and

"IT WAS A LONG AND PHYSICALLY INTENSE EXPERIENCE. THE FIRST PART OF THE MOVIE WAS SHOT IN THE WOODS, AND WE LITERALLY HIKED TO WORK IN THE MORNING. IT WAS GRUELING, BUT MORE THAN ANYTHING, I THINK IT WAS EXHILARATING. THE ENTIRE COMPANY WENT TO THE HUNGER GAMES AND FELT A PART OF THE ARENA." — GARY ROSS

GARY ROSS LOOKS ON
AS JENNIFER LAWRENCE
STRINGS A BOW.

then returning to the Capitol scenes before and after the Games.

As in most movies, the scenes were not shot in chronological order, which meant that the *Hunger Games* team had to keep careful track of how the actors and backgrounds looked in each frame, to ensure continuity in the final film. It also meant that the team was moving across North Carolina, shooting in place after place, all summer long.

Alli Shearmur of Lionsgate says, "I went to North Carolina every few weeks during the filming — it wasn't a typical situation. Gary had to make sure he had the footage he needed for every single scene, because there would be no time to reshoot later if he missed something. The movie would be in theaters in March 2012, ten months after shooting began. Because of this schedule, the production had to be unbelievably well choreographed and well rehearsed, and everybody worked long days to get what they needed there and then. They were in the woods for a long time, because they weren't going back."

The actors playing the tributes had already been through training together, but filming was a different kind of experience, eerily reminiscent of the Games themselves. Producer Jon Kilik says, "Once the kids were selected and they all came together, it was not so different from the Hunger Games. They were brought into this world; they were a little suspicious of each other, a little competitive with

GARY ROSS AND JENNIFER LAWRENCE
WORK ON A SCENE IN THE ARENA.

each other. And they were performing. They had to survive. Then they slowly started to work together, get to know each other, and they really embraced and embodied their characters beautifully."

The young actors filmed the first Cornucopia scene almost right away, and their training made

they needed them. Putting their training into practice brought the group closer together, and made them think about the story, too.

One highlight of the shooting was a visit from author Suzanne Collins. The actors were overjoyed — and awed — to have her on hand as they filmed

"IT WAS THE MIDDLE OF SUMMER AND IT WAS REALLY, REALLY HOT AND IT RAINED EVERY SINGLE DAY FOR AT LEAST AN HOUR. . . . FOR A LOT OF US, IT'S OUR FIRST FILM. WE'RE IN THE TRENCHES, WE'RE COVERED IN MUD, WE'RE FIGHTING AND SWEATING AND WE DON'T EVEN CARE. WE'RE JUST HAPPY TO BE HERE." — LEVEN RAMBIN

it go smoothly. Their moves were choreographed ahead of time, and stunt trainers were on hand if

one of the movie's pivotal scenes. Collins recalls, "I was on the set for Rue's death. The scene's so key, not only because of its emotional impact on Katniss — Rue's essentially become Prim's surrogate in the arena — but because it has to be powerful enough to trigger the first rumblings of the rebellion. It's very demanding for the actors. All three of the kids — Jen, Amandla, and Jack — they gave terrific performances. T-Bone Burnett had come up with this lovely, haunting melody for the lullaby. And Gary, who was, of course, masterminding the whole thing, filmed it beautifully. There's this one shot of Katniss cradling Rue in the periwinkle with the lush background of the forest. On the monitor it looked like an exquisite portrait, like something you'd frame and hang in a museum. I remember Amandla came and sat next to me between takes and she asked me, 'So, what did you imagine it would be like?' And I said, 'Like that.' But really, it exceeded my expectations."

Leven Rambin, who plays Glimmer, remarks on another notable aspect of the shoot. "It was an extreme experience to be out in the middle of nowhere with no electricity or Internet service or anything. It definitely felt like you were there — like you were really there. We were really hot — just dying out there — and isn't that really the point?"

"Our shooting schedule was crazy!" says Josh Hutcherson. "We were shooting three to four pages a day, which doesn't sound like much, but when you realize how many shots you have to have for each one of those things, it's an incredible amount." Like the tributes in the Games, the actors were exhausted at the end of every shooting day. And then they had to deal with the elements.

Summers in North Carolina are hot and humid — and wet. "We shot the arena section in state forests in North Carolina during the rainy season," Jon Kilik says. "It rained almost every afternoon but we rarely stopped. It was a very physically challenging film."

AMANDLA STENBERG PERCHES IN A TREE WITH THE HELP OF A FEW CREW MEMBERS.

Alli Shearmur remembers: "Joe Drake and I were there the day that Gary shot the aftermath of the tracker-jacker scene, when Katniss thinks she sees Peeta, then hallucinates that she sees Caesar Flickerman. They were doing a tremendous amount of work — and then the skies opened up. There was a torrential downpour. Everyone just stood around in their rain ponchos, cheerful as could be, because this was happening to them every day, and they knew it would stop soon. After the rain stopped, the mud was ankle-deep, and then it was like, 'Everybody! Take your places!' like it was no big deal at all."

TOP: THE CREW SHELTERS FROM THE RAIN.
BOTTOM: THE CREW PREPS FOR A SCENE IN
THE DUPONT STATE FOREST.

Jennifer Lawrence comments on the heat: "My Games costume was great in the fitting. It was perfect. As soon as we took it out in the hundred-and-something-degree weather, though, the leather jacket and the pants and the boots were quite different." Still, the team kept to a strict schedule, shooting through the rain and the heat and the mud — and watching out for other potential obstacles, too.

"We had a snake wrangler — a full-time snake wrangler — on set," Nina Jacobson points out. "We had a lot of bears. One place we shot in — North Fork, North Carolina — has one of the highest per-acre bear populations of any place in the United States."

Not all of the animals were dangerous, but most of them were a nuisance — especially the wild turkeys. "We had wild turkeys on the set where the Cornucopia was," recalls Isabelle Fuhrman, who plays Clove. "We'd be in the middle of a shot and the turkeys would come in and they'd send the ADs and PAs to chase them away. One day after work, we were driving home and we saw the turkeys on the pedestals on the Cornucopia — like they were having their own Hunger Games!"

Alli Shearmur remembers the experience of watching Ross shoot at night. "The woods where they shot the arena scenes were pristine. Untouched.

> "ONE DAY AFTER WORK, WE WERE DRIVING HOME AND WE SAW THE TURKEYS ON THE PEDESTALS ON THE CORNUCOPIA — LIKE THEY WERE HAVING THEIR OWN HUNGER GAMES!"

They hadn't been used for a movie since *The Last of the Mohicans*. The crew would bring in equipment on ATVs, sometimes put a scene together overnight. It appeared to be spontaneous, but there was an enormous amount of effort behind the scenes. I was there the night they shot the scene with the mutts. In the woods . . . in the dark . . . it was unbelievable."

Ross spent time with each of the actors, digging to the core of their characters. As Ross knew, an actor who understood his or her character could more easily be that person in front of the camera. The young actors, especially, were grateful for his careful approach.

"We did the scene where I was dying," says Amandla Stenberg, "and I was talking to Gary about it, because I thought I'd be sobbing my eyes out. But he decided I shouldn't be crying so much because my character was trying to be brave for Katniss, and that was really the start of the rebellion."

Wes Bentley plays Seneca Crane in the movie. He says, "When you're playing a character that's not as defined as the others, you really look to your

JENNIFER LAWRENCE PREPARES TO PRACTICE SNARES IN THE TRAINING CENTER.

director. Gary and I talked about Seneca being this sort of cocky kid who's never had anything bad happen to him in his life. He's just had success after success, climbing the ladder."

After their conversations, Ross watched Bentley closely, trying to remind him of what they'd discussed without destroying the momentum of any particular take. "Gary has such an amazing ability to feel the energy of a particular actor, to see the struggles you're having at any moment, and to set you on the right path without you really knowing what just happened," Bentley adds. "Gary understands the lens; he understands the performances; he understands the whole film as he's putting it together."

Dayo Okeniyi agrees. "Working with Gary is amazing because he has a way of making the set very calm, of making the actors feel comfortable. It feels like an indie set, being on this movie, very homey and family oriented. Gary doesn't put pressure on the take. He's just very light with it. *Do this; try that; no, that's not working, let's try it again.* He's very much like the script is the skeleton and as an actor it's your job to put the flesh on that."

Ross's approach set the tone for everything the actors did together. It could have felt arduous, but instead the shooting felt joyful and exciting. "It isn't always the case where you're in a constant state of laughter and merriment on a set," says Woody Harrelson. "But it was on this one."

"We were avid readers on the set," says Alli Shearmur. "Gary, Jennifer, Nina. Everyone. I bought Jennifer the collected works of J. D. Salinger for her birthday. There was a real family feeling there. Josh hosted Saturday night barbecues for the cast, and everybody was always playing basketball. One night, when T-Bone Burnett was there, Gary hosted a dinner for him. Jennifer's assistant and good friend, Justine, brought her guitar, played it beautifully

but kind of shyly, and, before you knew it, T-Bone Burnett was playing, too."

The actors playing the tributes developed a special bond. Leven Rambin says, "For a lot of us, it's our first film. We're in the trenches, we're covered in mud; we're fighting and sweating and we don't even care. We're just happy to be here."

After shooting wrapped for the day, the tributes spent time exploring nearby areas, or just getting to know each other better. "Most of us are in the same hotel," explains Jacqueline Emerson, who plays Foxface.

> "THE SCRIPT IS THE SKELETON AND AS AN ACTOR IT'S YOUR JOB TO PUT THE FLESH ON THAT."

"We go out to dinner every other night. We go to movies together. The other night I spent three or four hours just walking around with Jack and Dayo. We went to this great little bookstore and just hung out there."

"When we're doing all the scenes in the woods where we're fighting, those other kids are actually our friends," Josh Hutcherson points out. "You're used to hanging out and laughing with them, so it's kind of a weird transition when they say 'Action!' and suddenly there's a giant bloodbath."

While the actors were exploring their characters and their new friendships, other teams were putting the pieces in place for the movie's action sequences.

Location manager Todd Christensen had found the perfect place to film the scene where a wall of fire comes at Katniss, cornering her. "DuPont State Forest let us do a controlled burn, not only on their forest but about a quarter of a mile from the ranger's house. For Katniss to feel like she was trapped, they put in a tree that they ratcheted so it could come

GARY ROSS WORKS WITH ISABELLE
FUHRMAN AND JACQUELINE EMERSON
IN THE TRAINING CENTER.

down, but then she also had to fall into a rock. We had the tree — not the rock — so they put a rock in to make the drama of the scene better."

Then special effects foreman Brandon McLaughlin rigged a wire to make it appear as if fireballs were shooting at Katniss. "It's what we normally do when a director says, 'I want this to go from Point A to Point B and hit it every time,'" he explains. "There's a sixteen-inch cable right down the middle of the fireball, and we shoot it down a wire with what looks like a slingshot. The fireball

> "THERE'S A SIXTEEN-INCH CABLE RIGHT DOWN THE MIDDLE OF THE FIREBALL, AND WE SHOOT IT DOWN A WIRE WITH WHAT LOOKS LIKE A SLINGSHOT."

itself was a steel apparatus — like a giant cork-screw — with a product wrapped on top of it that we could ignite and burn." Any signs of the rigging would be erased in postproduction.

Another special effects challenge was building — and then destroying — the pyramid of Career Tributes' supplies. McLaughlin remembers that he

THE CREW PREPARES TO SHOOT THE FIREBALL SEQUENCE IN THE ARENA.

didn't discuss the pyramid in great depth with Gary Ross before he began setting it up. "We put something together to show him. What we thought was fairly good in size. And Gary said, 'I want it four times bigger.' So our eyes lit up, and we went back to the drawing board and we came up with something for him. He absolutely loved it."

When the pyramid's size increased, the size of the eventual explosion increased, too. Location manager Christensen hoped that wasn't going to be a problem. "The pyramid was built at North Fork in the same meadow as the Cornucopia. That's a watershed, and they don't want anything going into the water. We had to not only have that pyramid in a particular place, but also far enough away from the water, and blowing up away from the water. But it kept getting bigger! When I told the conservancy that our plans had changed — that the explosion would be larger — they were great. They just said, 'I wish we could be there to see it.' But they were busy doing other things."

Some scenes were too large or too complex to film in real places or with real actors, but these scenes could be extended with computer imaging. "When I'm choosing locations," production designer Phil Messina says, "I'm often thinking about which parts get set-extended, and where the extensions could start. You have to think of the entire frame, and

some of it is virtual. For the Avenue of the Tributes, it was just kind of a no-brainer that it was going to have to be a virtual environment. So I created the chariots and I designed the space — about a mile, from one end to the other, ending with the president's box. We just picked out the pieces we really needed to build — that's what made the most sense."

Visual effects like the rest of the Avenue, or the hologram in the Games Center, would be added after the movie was finished filming (and are being added as this book is being written). They will add texture and depth to many scenes, and create parts of the scenes that would be impossible to film.

Hovercraft concept
#7
A. Jaeger ILM 11.01.11

new door/stair position

TOP: AN IMAGE OF THE REAPING SCENE FROM ABOVE.
BOTTOM: A DIGITAL CONCEPT OF A CAPITOL HOVERCRAFT.

One final dimension to the film, of course, is the music. The movie's haunting and memorable score was composed by musical legend James Newton Howard. Just like the production design, the music hits two particular notes: the past and the future.

Ross describes James Newton Howard as "One of the greatest composers in movies. Somebody who's written some of the greatest scores. I think he's worked on over a hundred movies — his body of work speaks for itself."

Katniss's lullaby sprang to life when T-Bone Burnett read the lyrics in Suzanne Collins's book, says Gary Ross. "Suzanne's lyrics were iconic within the story already. Katniss sings the lullaby to Prim in the beginning and to Rue later in the movie. T-Bone went away one night and called me the next morning, saying, 'You're not going to believe this.' He was so thrilled. And then when I heard it, what was remarkable was it felt like it had always been there. It felt like something that came out of Appalachia that mothers had been singing to their kids for generations."

With months of filming, and many additional layers of postproduction work, the movie was finally ready to show to the larger world.

A DIGITAL CONCEPT OF A CAPITOL HIGH-SPEED TRAIN.

Train track concept
#2
A. Jaeger / C. Alzmann
low angle side view
ILM 11.01.11

PART 6

THE
LEGACY
OF
THE
HUNGER
GAMES

In *The Hunger Games* there's something for everyone.

A gripping adventure.

A political commentary.

A love story.

A cautionary tale.

Some call it science fiction, some call it potential reality.

Some say it's for teenagers, some say it's for adults.

The book — and now the film — captures themes and concerns that seem timely.

But its real strength, in the end, is that it's timeless. It speaks to us today and it will still speak — even more powerfully — tomorrow.

Director Gary Ross says, "*The Hunger Games* gets people invested in a contest. People are rooting for their favorites, rooting for their survival. And suddenly, unwittingly, the people being oppressed

> **"THE WAY YOU GET TO CONTROL PEOPLE IS TO MAKE THEM PARTICIPATE, NOT JUST SUBJUGATE THEM."**

are actually engaged in this form of entertainment. That's one of the things Suzanne did that was so brilliant. She understood the ultimate extension of something like this. The way you get to control people is to make them participate, not just subjugate them. If there's one survivor, one victor, we get them participating in our system."

It's one of the tricky questions about making *The Hunger Games* into a movie, of course. In a *New York Times* interview, Suzanne Collins wondered about this herself. "When you go to see the movie, you'll be a part of the audience in the theater, but will you feel like part of the Hunger Games audience as well? Will you actively be

KATNISS AND PRIM EMBRACE THE MORNING OF THE REAPING.

KATNISS HEADS TOWARD HER PRIVATE
SESSION WITH THE GAMEMAKERS.

ACKNOWLEDGMENTS

Thank you to the cast and crew of *The Hunger Games* for giving their time and sharing their memories so generously.

Thank you to Gary Ross, Nina Jacobson, and Jon Kilik for truly taking readers behind the scenes with their stories.

Thank you to Yon Elvira and Amanda Maes — this book would not have been possible without your help. And to the rest of the amazing team at Lionsgate: Tim Palen, Alli Shearmur, Joe Drake, Julie Fontaine, Kate Hubin Piliero, Rob McEntegart, David Nonaka, Douglas Lloyd, Michael Farmer, and Tanya Wolkoff.

Thank you to the miracle workers at Scholastic: David Levithan, Lindsay Walter, Rick DeMonico, Paul Banks, Sheila Marie Everett, and especially the ever-patient Emily Seife.

And thank you to Suzanne Collins, whose genius infuses every page of this book.

— K.E.

KATNISS GETS ONE
LAST LOOK AT CINNA
BEFORE BEING BROUGHT
UP TO THE ARENA.

rooting for certain tributes to live or die? Or will you distance yourself from the experience? How much will you be caught up in the Capitol's Game? I can't even answer that question for myself yet, but I'm really intrigued by it."

It's not every movie that makes you question the experience of watching it in the first place, but that is a part of the genius of the series. From the very start, it was willing to grapple with serious subjects within the framework of a compelling story. Collins deliberately constructed Panem with echoes of the world we live in, and these echoes reverberate in every moment of the film.

As Collins told the *New York Times*, "It's crucial that young readers are considering scenarios about humanity's future, because the challenges are about to land in their laps. I hope they question how elements of the books might be relevant in their own lives. About global warming, about our mistreatment of the environment, but also questions like: How do you feel about the fact that some people take their next meal for granted when so many other

> "THIS IS A GIRL WHO STARTS A REVOLUTION. THIS IS A GIRL WHO CHANGES THE WORLD!"

people are starving in the world? What do you think about choices your government, past and present, or other governments around the world make? What's your relationship to reality TV versus your relationship to the news? Was there anything in the book that disturbed you because it reflected aspects of your own life, and if there was, what can you do about it? Because you know what? Even if they're not of your making, these issues and how to deal with them will become your responsibility."

Like the next books in the series, the next films will show what happens when Katniss tackles some

of these questions in her own life and begins to face the consequences.

As Gary Ross sees it, "Katniss begins the Games as someone who only fights for her own survival. But she ends the Games as someone who's willing to give her own life for something bigger."

What else would she die for? Jennifer Lawrence smiles, saying, "You have to remember — this is a girl who starts a revolution. This is a girl who changes the world!"

President Snow has been worried all along, Ross points out. From the moment Katniss shot the apple out of the pig's mouth, he's known Katniss was trouble. Anyone capable of defying authority like that was capable of defying him. Now the worst has happened. The Hunger Games — meant to keep the districts and their people in line — have been turned against him.

Ross says, "Snow realizes this girl is a huge threat. He can't kill her, he can't get rid of her — and yet at the same time he can't live with her. That's why the second book begins with their relationship ratcheted up to such a great degree."

The next films in the series promise graver danger for Katniss.

Rebellion.

Revenge.

Tragic loss.

True love.

But the heart of the story remains the same. "Her ultimate strength is her strength of character," Ross points out.

In future films, this mockingjay will soar.